WE DON'T SPEAK ABOUT MOLLIE

VICKY JONES
CLAIRE HACKNEY

Hackney and Jones

HACKNEY & JONES

Acknowledgments

Special mention to Mark Romain for all the police procedural advice and input.

Visit his website:
https://www.markromain.com/

Contents

About Vicky Jones

Vicky Jones was born in Essex, England. She is an author and singer-songwriter, with numerous examples of her work on iTunes and YouTube. At 20 years old she entered the Royal Navy. After leaving the Navy realising she was drifting through life with no sense of direction, she wrote a bucket list of 300 things to achieve which took her traveling, facing her fears and going for her dreams. At the time of printing, she is two-thirds of the way through her bucket list.

One item on her list was to write a song for a cause. Her anti-bullying track called "House of Cards" is now on iTunes to download.

Writing a novel was on her bucket list, and through a chance writing competition at her local writing group, the idea for *Meet Me At 10* was born. Vicky hopes she can change hearts and minds due to some of the gritty themes of the book.

Vicky is a keen traveler, stemming from her days traveling the world in the Royal Navy, and has visited around 50 countries so far. She has also graduated from The Open University after studying part time for her degree in psychology and criminology—another bucket list tick! She is currently writing a book series about her bucket list adventures, the first of which is entitled *'Project Me, Project You'*, alongside planning and writing more fiction books and book marketing guides for self-published authors.

Also in the pipeline is a writing course, put together to help aspiring authors plan and write their first novel.

She now lives in Cheshire, splitting her time between there and visiting her family and friends back in Essex.

For more information on upcoming book releases, to tell us what you think of the books, or just to say hi, visit the sites below:

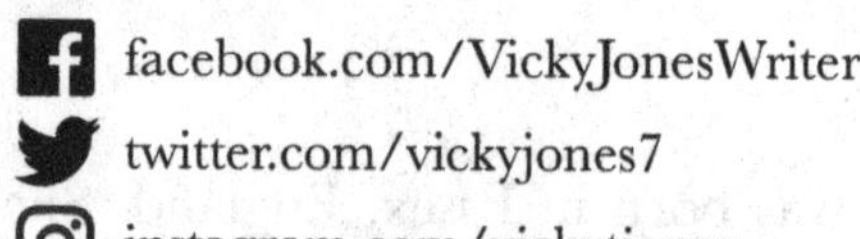

facebook.com/VickyJonesWriter

twitter.com/vickyjones7

instagram.com/vickytjones

About Claire Hackney

Claire Hackney is a former English Literature, Drama and Media Studies teacher who, after attending a local writing group with Vicky and writing several of her own short stories over the years, has now decided to focus her career on full-time novel writing.

She is an avid historian and has thoroughly enjoyed researching different aspects of the 1950s for the 'Shona Jackson' trilogy of novels.

Claire is very much looking forward getting started on the many future writing projects she and Vicky have in the pipeline, including the 'DI Rachel Morrison' thriller series and several standalone novels.

For more information on upcoming book releases, to tell us what you think of the books, or just to say hi, visit the sites below:

facebook.com/ClaireHackneyAuthor

twitter.com/clairehac

instagram.com/clairehackneyauthor

Grab your free book NOW

Instructions:

1. Open the camera or the QR reader application on your smartphone.

2. Point your camera at the QR code to scan the QR code.

3. A notification will pop-up on screen.

4. Click on the notification to open the website link

Book 1: The Burying Place

One high-profile case. No leads. No witnesses. No body. Amanda Walker's mother is missing. Detective Inspector Rachel Morrison has no leads on the case and time is running out. Amanda appeals to the public, but when no one comes forward, she chooses to immerse herself within a murderous underground group she believes is responsible for her mother's disappearance. But will the group believe Amanda's cover story?

Grab your free book NOW

Chloe - A prequel to Meet Me at 10

What if a life-shattering family tragedy forces you to completely rethink your future? Destined for a different path in life, twenty-year-old Chloe Bruce's world is shattered after a tragic accident on her father's plantation in Alabama.

Ok, so how do I get my FREE book?

EASY! See the next page

Grab your free book NOW

Instructions:

1. Open the camera or the QR reader application on your smartphone.

2. Point your camera at the QR code to scan the QR code.

3. A notification will pop-up on screen.

4. Click on the notification to open the website link

WE DON'T SPEAK
ABOUT MOLLIE

Prologue

THE LITTLE BOY ran as if seconds from death. As he squelched through the mud as fast as his thin, short legs could carry him, the wind on the heather-coated Scottish moors jabbed its spiky claws into the soft skin of his face. It was pitch black in every direction, the sodden ground beneath his mud-splattered Nike trainers the only certainty as to what lay ahead. The last light he could remember seeing was the amber glow of the taxi's interior light. "Car won't make it up that dirt track in the dark. Not with those waterlogged potholes," the driver had said after driving him from the tiny train station in Crailach village. "But head straight up for about a hundred and fifty yards after the cattle grid, and you can't miss the farmhouse."

Icy cold sheet rain hit his skin like needles the second the boy had gotten out of the Volvo, matting his curly brown hair to sharp, dripping wet shards across his forehead. Finally, fifty yards after he'd stepped carefully over the slippery cattle grid, his longed-for destination was in sight. Almost crawling the last hundred yards, he collapsed exhausted at the front door of a cottage situated in the middle of nowhere. The tiny fragment of moonlight that peeked through the only crack in the storm clouds above glinted off the windscreen of an old tractor parked in the front yard.

Blinking through the rivulets of water running down his frozen face, the boy staggered up the driveway to the black-painted oak front door of the farmhouse and hammered on it. He hopped from foot to foot and wrapped his arms around himself as he waited for someone to answer. After what felt like an age, a light illuminated the window to the side of the door.

"Who's banging on my door at this time of night?" a sharp female voice called from behind the door.

"N-n-n-n-n-an," the boy said, his teeth chattering uncontrollably in his mouth and rattling like Scrabble tiles in a bag. "It's me. Robbie."

The door opened and a woman, easily into her sixties, appeared in the hollow. She was wrapped in a thick navy blue dressing gown and holding a lantern torch. She shone it unapologetically in the boy's face, causing him to flinch as his small brown eyes reacted to the bright light. He lifted his arm to cover his face and lowered his head.

"That's nay possible. My Rab's only a bairn. Can nay be more than ten." The old woman reached out a bony, callused hand. "Put yer arm down, ween. I can nay see yer face."

"It's me, Nanny Morag. I swear down," the boy said, sniffing. He lowered his arm and stared at her, his brown eyes now adjusted to the light that was being shone in them. The old woman let her wrinkly blue eyes inspect his face and nodded.

"As I live and breathe. It is. What in God's name are yer doing up here on yer own, so far from home?" Her eyes wide, she looked behind him and all around, looking for a vehicle.

"Something really bad's happened, Nan," was all Robbie could squeeze out of his freezing cold mouth.

Chapter 1

"I'm sorry for your loss, Katie. Your aunt was truly a beautiful person inside and out."

Katie Spencer looked up from the worn beige carpet of her aunt's simply decorated living room. The walls were covered in textured off-white Superfresco, and had a burgundy and gold-trimmed paper border. The cream coloured sofa had been pushed back against the longest wall of the room to make a large space for mourners who had come back to the house for the wake. They held drinks and paper plates, laden with sandwiches and sausage rolls, and for a moment or two, Katie, with a glazed look, watched as they mingled sombrely with each other. Her brown eyes refocused on the kindly face of the old lady staring at her, who was dressed similarly in black. "Thank you, Doris. And thank you for helping me organise everything with the funeral. I'm not sure I could have done it on my own."

Doris laid a veiny hand on Katie's shoulder. "She was my younger cousin. It was the least I could do. Should have been me that went first, being ten years older." She shook her head. "Poor Joan. I saw her the day before the brain haemorrhage. She seemed fine. Moaning on about the bin men coming a day late, and all that mess the seagulls had made with the chip papers from it. But then, poof." Doris blew on her wrinkly fingers. "It was like the lights had simply just gone out. I'm just glad she didn't suffer."

"Me too. She wouldn't have liked being in a hospital. Too independent, she was. And she wouldn't have been able to survive without her daily walks along the seafront." Katie's eyes drifted over to the front bay window, through which she had a perfect view of the grey-white flint pebbles on Brighton beach that was just across the road from the house. The early afternoon sun glinted off the ice-blue sea in the distance. "Would have sent her loopy." She sighed and scanned the room.

Over by the grey stone fireplace, there was a group of black-suited men quietly talking to each other. Periodically, they raised their whiskey glasses when someone recalled a funny story about Joan Spencer. Sitting in overstuffed brown recliners around a small coffee table were two women. One of them, a slim woman of around thirty, with blonde hair and watchful blue eyes, sat with her daughter on her lap. The other woman, middle-aged, with brown hair and a plump but kind, open face held a small black and brown Yorkshire terrier. The little girl was dressed in a white blouse with ruffled sleeves, a black school skirt and shiny black Velcro shoes. In her dark brown bobbed hair was a thick black ribbon tied in a bow on the top. She reached out a thin pale hand and patted the dog, who whimpered and snuggled underneath it.

"It's nice that your older sister and her little daughter could make it down here for the funeral. It's been a while since you've seen each other, isn't it?" Doris asked.

Katie followed Doris's gaze over to the recliners. The little girl was now holding the terrier and trying to feed it half a sausage roll. "We're not close. It looks like Charlotte has made a new friend though. Timmy seems to have really taken to her."

"Poor thing. He hasn't really been eating since Joan died,"

Doris said. She dabbed her eyes with an embroidered handkerchief. "I'd better go and do the rounds."

She left Katie and shuffled over to the small group of men by the fireplace, picking up a tray of vol-au-vents from the table as she passed it. One man, tall and dark-haired, with bright green eyes, broke away from the pack and sidled up behind Katie. He wrapped his thick arms around the waistband of her black suit trousers and hugged her close to him.

"How are you holding up, babe?"

Katie turned to face her boyfriend. "I'm OK, I guess. It feels weird, though, Auntie Joan not being here. She lived in this house all her life. Me too, pretty much. And now? Oh, Tom. It's like losing mum all over again." For the first time, Katie felt the tears prick at the corners of her eyes. She pressed her face into his broad shoulder, making the soft fabric of his black suit damp.

"It's OK, darling. I know how much she meant to you. Why don't we mill around for a bit? There are some people who have a long drive back home, so might need to go soon. It's almost two."

Katie lifted her face out of Tom's shoulder and looked over at the carriage clock on the mantelpiece. "Is it that time already?"

Guided by Tom, Katie walked around the small living room, stopping to chat to each little group. Smiling and replying in all the right places, she couldn't shake the cloying weight on the back of her head from her sister's penetrative glare.

A little voice piped up through the dull burr of voices. "Mummy, can I take Timmy for a walk along the beach? Please? Oh please?"

"Not right now, Charlotte," came Jenny's stern reply.

———

Tom watched on as Katie talked to another mourner.

"It's a lovely spread, dear," the curly-permed old lady said to Katie as she scooped up another two triangle sandwiches and placed them on her china plate. "Joan, Doris and I used to play bridge with the ladies down at the community centre. Youngest one there, she was. Do you remember me?"

Katie smiled and nodded. "Yes, of course I remember you, Violet. Auntie Joan said you taught her all the tricks of the trade." She tapped the end of her nose.

"Never lost a match, us two. I wouldn't have wanted to play with anyone else. Doubt I'll play again." Violet clasped her arthritic fingers around the plate, which wobbled slightly in her grasp. "She loved you so much, though, dear. As if you were her own. After you moved down here when you were not much older than that little one over there," she pointed to Charlotte. "Joan never thought of herself as your aunt. She saw you as her daughter."

"I know, Violet. I'm going to miss her so much." Katie sniffed and dabbed at her eyes.

"How's the studying going? It's nursery teaching you're going in for, isn't it?"

Katie blushed. "Yes. Yes it is. I'm loving it. It's my dream to have my own nursery one day. I wished Auntie Joan could be there to see me graduate next year. She's the one who encouraged me to go on the college course. I would never have had the guts to believe in myself enough to apply."

Tom rushed over holding a fresh tissue. "Here, babe. It's OK." He wrapped his arms around her and kissed her on the cheek.

"Oh, you two are so sweet together. So, will it be little ones for you two soon then? I remember Joan mentioning that you were trying, and I've not seen a couple more in love than you two," Violet gushed as she reached out to stroke Tom's arm.

"Hopefully, fingers crossed," Tom replied.

As Katie excused herself to fix her makeup in the downstairs toilet, Tom continued, in more hushed tones this time. "It's taking a bit longer than we'd originally hoped it would, but that could be down to stress, you know. I've taken a few less shifts at the boatyard, but now, with Joan passing away, we might need to take it easy for a while. Just to let Katie adapt to life without the only mum she's known since she was seven. Poor thing, she didn't have the easiest of starts in life. So we want to get it absolutely right with our first one."

"That girl has had more than her fair share of heartache, you can't argue with that. Only five when her own mum died, then having to split from her sister and move down here all alone a couple of years later, when her dad couldn't cope with raising them both on his own up in Liverpool. I mean, that has to have an effect on you. Joan was the only stability that girl has ever known. Well, until you came along, young Thomas." Violet linked her arm with his.

"I'd give her the world if I could. She'll be an amazing mum, I just know it." Tom gazed adoringly at Katie as she re-entered the living room, fresh makeup applied to her eyes. "You OK, babe?" he asked as she walked back over.

"I'm fine now. Just needed a moment."

"It was a beautiful service," a voice sounded behind them. Katie turned to meet the cold, blue eyes of her sister. She was similarly dressed in a black trouser suit and a black blouse with white edging. Her mid-length blonde hair was poker straight and her makeup pristinely applied. Only three years older than Katie, Jenny looked at least twice that, with her heavily applied foundation barely covering the lines around her nose and mouth.

"Hi, Jenny. Thank you for coming down. I know it's a long journey for you and Charlotte." Katie looked over Jenny's shoulder to see Charlotte walking up to them. She stopped by Jenny's side and reached up to grab her hand.

"The thought that's gone into everything. Every little detail. Aunt Joan would have been proud of you." Jenny paused to pick a piece of lint off her shoulder, inspect it and flick it away.

"That's all down to Katie here. A bit OCD, but I love her

for it. How are you doing, Jenny? How's old scouse land?" Tom added.

Jenny's eyes didn't lift from Katie, and vice versa. "It's fine, Tom. I can't stay down here for long though. I've got the yoga studio to sort, you know?"

Katie and Jenny stood with fixed smiles on their faces. Tom looked between them both, the cool atmosphere between them tangible.

"Right then, I'll leave you two to catch up. Orange juice, was it, babe?" Tom waited for Katie to nod before relieving her of her empty glass and heading over to the kitchen, linking arms with Violet as he moved away.

"That's a shame you can't stay. How long has it been since we last spoke properly? Five? Six years?" Katie asked. She looked down at Charlotte and smiled. "This one was a tiny baby in the photo I've got of her. Look how you've grown. I like your ribbon." She reached down to stroke her hand over her niece's silky brown hair, but Jenny clasped Charlotte's hand tighter and ever so slightly pulled her back.

"I know. But life gets in the way, you know."

"How's the business going?" Katie asked, determined to crack the thick layer of ice between them. "I saw your pictures of the studio on Facebook. It looks amazing."

"It's doing really well. I have three sessions of yoga per week now. I get instructors coming in now too. We're still building, so there's always going to be some ups and downs. But I'll get there."

Katie smiled, radiating genuine warmth from her eyes. "I'm proud of you."

Jenny's smile was cooler. "Thank you. And this little monster just keeps on growing." She scooped Charlotte up in her arms and tickled her underneath her chin. It was the first sign of softness Katie had seen in Jenny throughout their stilted conversation. Charlotte giggled and squirmed in her grasp.

"She's grown so much. I'd love to get to know her." Katie reached out again but Jenny put Charlotte down.

"Go play," Jenny commanded of her daughter. Charlotte obeyed and ran back over to Timmy who was now lying in his basket by the fireplace.

"I know. But we both have such busy lives, and live at opposite ends of the country. So it wouldn't be practical," Jenny said.

Katie let out a long sigh. "Look, can you at least stay for a cuppa after everybody has gone? I'd really like to talk. I can't remember the last time we actually spoke properly. Texts don't count, and Facebook Messenger feels so impersonal. It's like I haven't heard your voice for so long. I'm all alone here now. Well, apart from Tom. But I could really use having my sister around right now."

"I've booked a hotel nearby and I need to check in soon to keep Charlotte to a routine."

Katie's eyes widened. "Cancel the hotel and stay here. Charlotte would love it. She's five minutes' walk from the beach. And she can walk Timmy with me. It'll be lovely to spend some time together." She beamed as the idea formed in words from her mouth before it had in her head.

Jenny remained stone-faced. "I think it's best the way it is. Charlotte is looking forward to her big breakfast in the hotel. I've told her they do chocolate pancakes. And today has been tough on her with being around so many strangers. She doesn't really understand why we've travelled all this way to the funeral of an old lady she never even met. I'm only letting her play with that old dog to keep her settled."

They both looked over to see Charlotte almost lying in the basket with Timmy, who didn't appear to mind.

Katie's optimistic expression faded. "OK then. I suppose that's for the best. For Charlotte. But maybe I could come over to the hotel tomorrow, before you leave?"

"Um... Yeah. Sure." Jenny slung her black Fendi handbag

over her shoulder and checked her watch. "We'd better be going. But thank you again for your hospitality."

"You're welcome. I'll see you out."

Katie walked a step behind Jenny, who'd scooped Charlotte out of Timmy's basket and brushed the dog hair off her once perfectly pressed, now crumpled, black skirt. She sat her on her hip as she opened the front door. "Bye, Katie."

Jenny's farewell bit into Katie's face as painfully as the stiff sea breeze that blew through the open door.

Chapter 2

DI Rachel Morrison stood in the foyer of Merseyside Police's headquarters. It was her first day in her new job and on her way into work that morning she'd taken a drive past the building and all around the city centre to acclimatise. She'd spent the rest of the morning in HR filling in forms and other induction paperwork and, given a half an hour break before meeting her new team, she'd decided to go for a breath of fresh air outside the building. After taking in a huge lungful of salty air drifting over from the Irish Sea, far out beyond the River Mersey, she'd walked across the busy main road to explore the pedestrian zones along the promenade. A few minutes along from the Albert Dock, the Royal Liver Building loomed large above her. The opposite-facing green copper cormorants, one on the top of each of the grey-white building's towers, had their wings raised as if protecting the sea and the city. This city was Rachel's new home. A world away from the bastite rocks of the wild Cornish coast she'd left behind, but not so dissimilar from where her career had begun at the Met Police, she thought as she wandered back along the pathway. Two of the docks in Liverpool, Canning and Wapping, shared their names with towns and boroughs in London, she noticed. There was even an area in the city called Kensington

—even though on her drive around it earlier she'd noticed the neighbourhood looked strikingly more deprived than its southerly counterpart. *It's a fresh start, though, just what I need,* she'd thought on her walk back across the road to the police headquarters, a massive eight-floor modern building with brown-red bricks and glinting windows.

Rachel's air of calm, collected authority was reinforced by the smart, navy blue tailored suit she was wearing. Smoothing down her long, dark brown hair, she stood up and reached out to shake the hand of the young detective sent down to the foyer to greet her.

"Detective Inspector Morrison, welcome. I'm Detective Constable Johnny Bradley. Now you're all finished over in HR, I'll show you up to your new office."

DC Bradley was in his early thirties, wearing a pristinely pressed dark blue three-piece suit with a striped blue and white tie. Tall and athletically built, he flashed her a set of bright white, perfectly straight teeth and with a tanned hand smoothed his sandy blond hair back into its shaped quiff. He held out his other arm to show the way to the lift.

Rachel smiled back. *I can see my face in those shiny black shoes of his,* she thought. *A good start.* "Lead the way, DC Bradley."

As they exited the lift on the floor where the Reactive Crime Unit was based, Bradley continued his tour. "So, the tea and coffee machines are located down that corridor there. Interview rooms down there, and toilets in there," Bradley pointed. "Canteen is back on the ground floor. But if you get lost then you can ask anyone. We're a friendly bunch. It's probably a bit bigger here than down in Lizard, right?" Bradley grinned.

"Well, I started my career in the Met, so I'm sure I'll readjust," Rachel said. Bradley's confident grin faded.

"Sorry, boss, forgot about that part of the briefing on your transfer up here," Bradley replied with an apologetic raise of his shapely eyebrows.

Rachel fixed him with an authoritative, but pleasant stare.

"First rule of detective work, Bradley. Check your facts. Now, let's crack on, shall we?"

"Yes, boss."

Bradley pushed open the door of the Reactive Crime Unit. There was a hive of activity going on inside. Phones were ringing, detectives were scribbling down notes and conversations around case whiteboards were being had. They walked through the centre aisle of the countless rows of desks until they reached the open door of a small partitioned cubicle. Inside there was a desk, bookshelves behind it and to the right of the room, and in the left was a rectangular table with four metal chairs with royal blue fabric seat covers tucked in underneath. A thick layer of dust gave the table top a dull, chalky appearance.

"Here we are. Sorry it's not been properly cleaned and organised already. We only had the briefing that you were coming up to join us last week. Thought we had longer. Don't you normally have to give a month's notice before transfer?"

"Normally. I asked to come up immediately." Rachel cast her mind back to her last day in Cornwall and the note left on her car window. She'd packed her stuff up that same week, her new accommodation in Liverpool hastily found. "Just needed last week to get myself moved into my new place so today was agreed as my start date."

"Fine by us. We could use the expertise you bring. We've heard all about the cases you boxed off down there. Bit of a legend, you, boss. I'll go and get some cleaning stuff and we'll get you settled in, shall we? I'll get you a coffee too."

"Thanks. Black, two sugars."

Bradley nodded and slipped past her, leaving her to take in her new surroundings. The cubicle was a few feet larger than her old one down in Lizard Police station, but it was hard to tell with the amount of old dusty files and paperwork piled up on the shelves that had seen better days. She leaned down and blew off the top layer of dust off her desk, then coughed.

"Rachel, hi. You made it up here in one piece, then?

Superintendent Graham Jenkins. We spoke on the phone." Jenkins held out a hand and shook Rachel's firmly.

He was in his early fifties, tall and thin, with his greying hair combed back neatly. His police uniform was as perfectly pressed as Bradley's suit was. *Clearly they have higher standards here*, Rachel thought, her mind drifting back to some of her former colleagues and their bacon grease-smothered ties and rounded bellies. Smiling, she remembered the one exception to this, PC Michelle Barlow, the only fast food junkie with a size eight waist she'd ever met.

"It's good to finally meet you, young lady," Jenkins said. He swept his hand horizontally across the air as if painting a newspaper headline on it. "The detective inspector who brought the Killer of Kynance Cove to justice. You've brought quite the reputation up with you. No pressure, eh?" Jenkins chuckled.

"No, sir, none at all," Rachel replied with a wry smile.

"When the Assistant Chief Constable heard about your recent success in Cornwall, solving the mystery of all those missing people, he thought you might be the ideal person to carry out a structured review on our own misper enquiries. To be honest, we've got a few problematic cases on the books, and it would be nice to have a fresh set of eyes on them as they seem to be going nowhere. We're hoping you can make some headway on a few of them, but even if you can't, the fact that we've bought in a specialist to carry out a stringent review will be very well received by the families when we call to give them their weekly update. Not to mention the good feeling we'll get on social media. Those faceless keyboard warriors can be brutal and do no end of damage to morale around here." He leaned in and his voice dropped to a conspiratorial whisper. "Between you and me, some of the families have been kicking up a bit of a stink, saying we haven't been putting enough effort into finding their loved ones for them, and your timely arrival will take a bit of pressure off us in that respect." Standing straight again, he offered her a sympathetic smile. "I appreciate that low and medium risk misper enquiries don't come under the purview of reactive crime, but you would be doing us a huge favour. We've allocated you a budget that will keep you going for a couple of months and, after that, we can see about getting you settled into a far meatier role. Robbery, perhaps? Or taking over as the DI for the main CID office? If you do well on this assignment, you'll be able to take your pick. Would you have any objections to doing that for us?"

Rachel had been in the job for long enough to know how these things worked. The ACC Jenkins reported to was obviously a very savvy operator. Having read Rachel's CV, he had seen a way to transform a gnarly situation into a great public relations success story. No doubt, there would be a press release in a day or two, announcing the formation of a new Task Force and crowing over the positive action the ACC had taken to improve the Force's success at tracing missing people. It would, no doubt, be loaded with the usual top brass type rhetoric, emphasising the ACC's undying commitment to provide the people of Merseyside with the best police service that money could buy. Her recruitment would probably be sold to the public as a sign of Jenkins' personal commitment to provide answers for the troubled families who were so desperate to know what had happened to their missing loved ones. And as for Jenkins asking her if she had any objections? Well, that was just him being polite. The police force was a disciplined service, not a democracy, and they both knew she would do exactly as she was told, whether she liked it or not. Still, it was nice of him to dress the order up as a request, and there was no point in being cynical about it, or in kicking up a stink. It was just the nature of the job.

"None, sir. Just happy to contribute in the best way I can around here," she said, toeing the party line. "I just hope I don't disappoint. I had a great team down in Cornwall. I can't take all the credit." Rachel's mind drifted back once again, to Amanda Walker and the sight of the gaping bullet hole in her forehead that still gave her cold sweats at night.

"Speaking of teams, let me introduce you to Detective Constable Maggie Chapman. She'll be assigned to you for the misper reviews. She's a very experienced officer."

Rachel looked over Jenkins' shoulder to see a plump, middle-aged woman, with spiky blonde hair and bright red lipstick, get up from her cluttered desk and walk over to them. She was dressed in a loose fitting black suit jacket, over a gaudy red and white stripy dress. A long chain hung around her neck, to which her red, horn-rimmed reading glasses were attached.

"Someone mention my name?" she trilled.

"DC Chapman, this is Detective Inspector Rachel Morrison, your new guv'nor," Jenkins said.

"Call me Mags, dear. Sorry, *boss*, I should say." Mags said in a soft scouse accent. "It's nice to finally meet you. We've heard a lot about you."

"So it would seem," Rachel replied, with a deep breath. "Nice to meet you too, Mags." Rachel held out her hand, which Mags shook.

"I think it'll be quite full on for the next couple of months, with what they want us to get through," Mags said, fingering the stems of her reading glasses.

"In what way?" Rachel replied.

Mags nodded over Rachel's shoulder. Rachel turned to face the mountain of files on her shelves. *Of course they'd be mine,* she thought with an inner eye roll. It struck her that there were an awful lot of files to get through in a two-month window, which was a tad concerning.

"We've had quite a few misper files piling up over the years, as you can see. God knows what's in them. It wouldn't surprise me if Lord Lucan and Shergar were in that lot somewhere." Mags snorted at her own joke, then straightened her face. "Nobody around here has had the time to properly go through those old folders. Let alone solve them. Yet." Mags grinned and clasped her hands across her middle.

Jenkins walked over to Rachel and placed a hand on her

shoulder. "I have every faith in you two. I couldn't have picked anybody better to box off these cases. And I'm going to enjoy my retirement in a few months knowing that all these loose ends are tied up."

Forcing a smile, and wondering what she had got herself into, Rachel walked around her desk and placed her hands on the back of her chair. "Well, we'd better get started then."

DC Bradley appeared at the door with a bucket of cleaning materials and a steaming black coffee. "First thing's first, though, boss," he said, holding out the coffee to Rachel.

———

KATIE HAD BEEN SITTING up in bed next to Tom for the last half an hour staring at a tiny crack on the far wall of their bedroom. Her fingers were wrapped in the cotton fabric of their pale blue duvet cover. Tom looked up at her and placed his book down on his chest.

"You OK, babe? You've been quiet for a while."

Katie looked down at him and sighed. "I just can't believe she's gone, Tom. She was more than just my aunt. I was too young to really remember my actual mum. Auntie Joan was my whole world for so many years. She cared for me more than my loser of a father. Couldn't even be arsed to pay his respects to his own sister at her funeral, when she stepped up to be both parents to me. Just because he couldn't handle being a dad. Oh, Tom, how did it come to this? I'm alone again in the world. Apart from you, that is."

"I know, baby. I know. You've always got me, no matter what. OK?" Tom pulled her down into a tight cuddle. He stroked her hair and kissed the top of her head. "I promise you, we'll get through this."

———

"How's my work mum this fine Tuesday morning?" a chirpy voice sounded from the end of Mags' cluttered, paper-strewn work desk. She looked up from her computer screen and pulled her reading glasses to the end of her nose. There she saw the smiling face of the young PC who had brought her another archive box up from the records office. He was barely twenty with short brown hair, a small scar on his upper lip and a twinkle in his blue eyes. He wore a tidy police uniform and had his Sillitoe striped cap resting on the top of the box.

"Oh, hello, Mick. I'm very well, thank you, sweetheart. How's that gorgeous girlfriend of yours?"

Mick perched on the end of Mags' desk and folded his arms. "Amazing. She's definitely a keeper, this one. Had a big bowl of scouse literally ready to eat as soon as I walked through the door last night. And a beer waiting. That girl is something special, I can tell you. And she'd remembered the match was on. Had Sky Sports 1 on already for when I sat down. Boss, that, eh?"

A huge grin swept across Mags's bright red lips. Her blue-grey eyes twinkled with pride. She had taken Mick under her wing as soon as he'd started as a newly trained PC in their department, and taken a keen interest in his private life. "Oh, I'm so pleased for you, darling. It's about time you had a good one."

Mick blushed. "I know. I've had some crazy ones, me, haven't I?" Mick looked to the heavens and grinned. "Remember the girl who only let me eat the orange jelly babies in the pack?"

Mags let out a bark of laughter. "Oh my God, yes. And the one after that who wanted you to ring her every half an hour, even if you were on the loo."

"Jesus. Thank God *that* didn't last. No, I think Lisa's different. Normal, you know?"

"Well then, you make sure you appreciate her," Mags said, jabbing him with her elbow.

"Of course I will." Mick stood up straight. He leaned in to

Mags. "I even did the washing up at half time," he whispered in her ear. "A changed man, I am."

Mags slapped him on his arm and laughed. "That's my boy. Now away with you. Momma's got work to do."

As Mick went to sit down at his desk over the far end of the office, he passed Rachel striding past who stopped at Mags' desk holding a blue cardboard folder.

"Looks like you're a lot of people's 'mums' around here," Rachel said, smiling.

Mags looked up at her. "Too many years of experience around here. I like to pass it on to the younger waifs and strays. Poor Mick over there never knew his parents. They died in a car crash just after he was born. Grew up in different foster homes. He's called me the 'mum he never had' since his first day here. I'm OK with that; no children of my own, you see." Sadness seemed to glaze over Mags' normally bright eyes. She snapped back into work mode. "If I can pass on that wisdom to the next generation then I'll be happy with that. Now, shall we get started on those files?"

"This one here I think could be an easy win." She held up the folder. "Hazel Connolly. I looked through the notes and then checked on the database. Her credit card was used last week, so I'm sending Bradley over to her house to confirm it's her and she's not missing after all. Looks like an admin error on this one. Database was updated, but not the paper file." She handed the folder to Mags who licked a finger and leafed through.

"An admin error? That's not like me." She spotted the amendment note Rachel had made in red pen by the 'bank cards last used' line. "Right, well, this looks like one less off the list."

Rachel took the folder back off her. "Means we'll have to take a more detailed look at the other folders cluttering up my office. Just to make sure they are all officially unsolved still." She looked pointedly at Mags, who lowered her eyes.

"Well, that's me told," she murmured with a forced smile.

"Just, if you wouldn't mind not mentioning it to the juniors on the team?" she whispered, nodding over to Bradley a couple of desks away who was staring intently at his computer screen and diligently making notes. "I've heard how smart you are, but there's really no need for you to show me up to assert yourself here."

"What do you mean?"

Mags spread her hands. "Well, you're this new supercop. Oh, I don't want to sound bitter there, dear. I'm just happy to make it to my retirement in nine months' time. I've got nothing left to learn in this job or to prove."

Rachel bristled. "I'm not looking for you to 'prove' yourself to me, Mags. Your thirty odd years' service shows me you've done that already. No, the mistake on this case was just an oversight, that's all. I'm not out to 'show anyone up'." She relaxed her face. "And if anything, *I* need to prove myself to you. Anyway, Superintendent Jenkins had nothing but good things to say about you when we first were introduced."

The corners of Mags' mouth twitched. "He just wants those cases boxed off. Tired of the flak he gets from above. He doesn't care how that happens and probably thinks flattery will get us to work quicker on them."

Chapter 3

KATIE STOOD OUTSIDE THE LARGE, white stone hotel a mile from Brighton town centre and took a deep breath. Her cordial, but frosty, interaction with her sister yesterday at the funeral had made her a little nervous. But seeing her niece Charlotte had reminded her that she did have a family, and Katie was determined to try and work on her fractious relationship with her older sister. She pushed open the glass front door of the hotel and walked over to the lifts. Her text from Jenny had told her to go to Room 364. When she located the correct corridor, she walked along the purple carpeted hallway and up to the door. With trepidation, she lifted her hand to knock.

"Oh. Hello," Jenny said. She was wearing her outdoor coat as if ready to leave and held the door open a few inches, looking thoroughly put out that Katie was stood there.

"Hi," Katie replied. "Can I come in?"

"Um... OK." Jenny opened the door to the hotel room.

Inside it was fairly spacious, with a big white quilted double bed in the middle of the room complete with purple runner, and a smaller single at the far end. On the double bed was a large open suitcase, half packed. Charlotte sat on her little single bed playing with a fluffy black and tan dog teddy. The silence hung like thunder clouds in the air between them.

"I brought you these," Katie said, holding out a bunch of multi-coloured tulips. "I remembered you saying they were your favourite last time we spoke on the phone."

"You have a good memory." Jenny took the flowers and laid them on the bed next to her handbag. "We'll be leaving soon. It's a long train ride back up to Liverpool."

Shit, Katie thought, looking down at the extra thing to carry that she had given Jenny. "Well, I just wanted to say thank you for coming down here to support me. It means a lot. And to see this little one too." Katie pointed at Charlotte, then took a few steps towards her. Charlotte looked up from her teddy.

"I've called him Timmy now," Charlotte said, holding out the teddy.

"Oh wow, he really looks like my auntie's dog, doesn't he? That's a great name. Do you remember me from yesterday, Charlotte?"

"Mummy told me you were her friend."

Katie felt her heart slice open. She looked behind her at Jenny, who looked away.

"It's best for her she doesn't get attached. You and I live so far apart. She needs stability at her age," Jenny said, the irony of her words to her exiled sister lost on her.

"Please stay a bit longer, Jenny. We can spend some time together. I know we've lost our connection, but we're si—."

"Charlotte, can you put your books in your Trunki, please?" Jenny cut in. She turned back to look at Katie. "I can't. The studio. I need to get back."

"What was your favourite toy when you were small?" Charlotte piped up. Katie looked down at her large brown eyes.

"Oh, um…" The question surprised Katie. "You know what, I can't really remember. I'll have to get back to you on that one. Your hair is beautiful. Brown like chocolate. Just like mine when I was your age. Can I brush it?" Katie leaned down to the bed and picked up Charlotte's soft-bristled pink brush.

"Yes, please," Charlotte said, swivelling round on the bed. Katie glanced at Jenny who stared at her. After three seconds of hair brushing, Jenny leaned into Katie and snatched the brush away.

"Charlotte, I have asked you once already to put your books in your Trunki. Please do as Mummy says," Jenny barked, making Charlotte jump.

"Yes, Mummy," Charlotte mumbled. She shuffled off the bed and over to her pile of books strewn across the hotel room floor and set about piling them into her little panda suitcase.

"I'm sorry, it's just, it's time to leave now," Jenny said as she zipped up her suitcase, not looking at Katie.

"It's OK," Katie replied in a quiet voice. She turned the little pink brush over and over in her hands. "I just miss Auntie Joan so much. I guess, except for you and the little one, all my family is gone. Well, apart from Dad, but it's been so long since I've heard from him." Katie put the brush down and reached into her handbag. She took out her phone and fished into the folds in the leather wrap case. "This is the only photo I have of him. It was taken years ago. I must have brought it with me when I was first sent here. He never calls, or writes, or texts. I don't even have his number." Katie stroked the photo with her thumb as she spoke.

Jenny sighed and looked over at Charlotte. A pensive look glazed over her face. "He's just…Dad, you know?"

Katie looked up from the photo, her eyes moist. "Does he ever ask about me?"

As the answer sat on Jenny's tight red lips, Charlotte's little voice piped up from the carpet. "Mummy, I can't close the buckle." Her face screwed up with exertion as she tried in vain to squeeze her little fingers around the plastic catch to press it into place.

"Here, sweetheart, let Mummy do it." Jenny sank down

beside Charlotte and closed the case after rearranging some of the books her daughter had tried to force in there. "I'm sorry I snapped at you," she whispered in Charlotte's ear. "Mummy's very tired, that's all."

"It's OK, Mummy. Can I play my game on your phone, please? Just for a few minutes? Please?"

"OK. But just until I've packed the rest of our things."

Charlotte wandered over to Jenny's handbag which was on the dressing table by the window.

Katie dabbed her eyes with a tissue and cleared her throat. "Can I use your loo before I go?"

"Sure," Jenny replied without looking up from Charlotte's Trunki.

Katie opened up the door to the en suite and closed it behind her. While she was in there, the voices in the bedroom seemed to change in tone. "Who is this, Mummy?" she heard Charlotte ask. Before Katie flushed the toilet, she opened the door a crack and looked into the bedroom. Charlotte was looking down at a small passport-sized photograph she'd found in the flap of Jenny's mobile phone case.

Jenny snatched the photo out of Charlotte's hand. "What are you doing going through my phone? You *never* go through Mummy's things, is that clear?" Jenny's eyes were raging.

Katie recoiled, then looked again through the crack in the door.

By now, Jenny had composed herself after seeing tears in Charlotte's frightened eyes. "I'm sorry, darling." Jenny sank to her haunches and rubbed her daughter's shoulder. She showed Charlotte the photo. "This little girl is called Mollie. But we don't speak about her. OK? It's important that you understand that, Charlotte. Don't ask about her again, OK?"

Charlotte blinked and looked at her mother. "Why?"

"We just don't. Now, go put on your shoes or we'll miss the train."

With a shrug, Charlotte trotted off to find her red trainers. Katie flushed the toilet and came out of the en suite, wiping her hands on the front of her jeans. "That's better. I was busting."

Jenny didn't look up from the carpet. She pocketed the photo and wiped her eyes with the heel of her palm.

"I was thinking. Maybe I could drive up one weekend and book a hotel? Have Charlotte overnight? I'd love to spend some quality time with her. And of course fulfilling my auntie duties of feeding her ice cream for breakfast and sweets for tea?" Katie aimed that last comment over her shoulder at Charlotte, who made an audible gasp of delight.

"She doesn't like strangers," Jenny replied. "Sorry. I didn't mean that to come out like that." She exhaled. "I meant, well, she doesn't know you."

"It's not for the want of trying, though, Jen. I write, I send cards, I send books and toys for her," Katie said. Her tolerance for her sister's cold and distant manner had run out. She set her lips. "Did you even give them to her?"

"I've been busy, I told you. I have my own life to lead, Katie. And so have you. I suggest we keep the two separate. For everyone's sake," Jenny hissed back. "Right, you," she directed at Charlotte, who was now wearing her trainers with the Velcro stuck down, and had buttoned up her pink duffel coat. "Time to go." Jenny walked over and opened the door. "I'll text you when we get home. Bye, Katie."

Chapter 4

"Bloody hell, I keep forgetting my pissing password to this thing," Mags said as she bashed her fingers into the buttons of her black computer keyboard. She wiggled the mouse and tutted loudly. It was late afternoon, the shadows long across her sun-bathed, coffee cup-cluttered work desk.

"I'll ring tech, see if they can reset it. Otherwise we won't have time to get started on these cases before you go home," Rachel said, reaching for Mags' desk phone.

"No, don't do that yet. I'm sure I've got it written down somewhere." Mags fished into her handbag and drew out an A5 sized ring-bound notebook.

"You write your passwords down?" Rachel said out of the corner of her mouth.

"Oh, no one's going to know what the words 'monkeysocks' and 'pebbledash' mean, now are they? Let alone con their way in here to hack into my computer. And people around here know better than to go in Momma's handbag," Mags added with a tap of her nose.

"Still, I think from now on you should really try to leave your passwords in your head, hmm? Just do what I do and make it something obvious to you and only you. Even if it's work related, like something you see in front of you every day when you sit at your desk."

Mags laughed. "Well, in that case my new password will be 'studmuffin', then, won't it?" She jutted her head to indicate DC Bradley who had just sat back down at his desk. He looked very smart in his tailored three piece suit and baby pink tie. His sandy brown hair was neatly combed, as usual, into a trendy quiff, his stubble beard immaculately trimmed. Mags caught his eye and waved at him.

"Mags," Rachel said, tutting, then smiling. "What about this password?"

"I think this might be this week's one." Mags tapped the d-o-n-k-e-y letters and hit the return key. "There we are." Her desktop flashed up, bright and clear.

Rachel looked down at the notepad Mags had leafed through to find her password. From inside it, a small bunch of holiday snaps had slipped out and landed in a heap on Mags' messy desk. "Wow, where was that one taken?" Rachel asked, picking one photo up.

Mags looked away from her computer screen and pulled her half-moon glasses to the tip of her nose to observe the photograph. "Oh, that one? That was in Brazil. That's my husband there, next to the palm tree. We're planning to live out there. We've already sized up some beachfront properties."

"That sounds amazing. What about that one?" Rachel said, pointing to another beach photograph. "Where was that taken?"

"That one was in Tahiti. We went on a cruise. Amazing, it was."

"Wow, you really have travelled, haven't you?"

"Certainly have. Right, let's find these files," Mags said, looking down her nose through her glasses as she scrolled across the cluttered desktop. She clicked on a folder. "Where are the buggers?" She closed down the wrong folder and tried another.

"Buggers?" Rachel said, raising an eyebrow.

"The cases. I can never remember which folder to open. Oh well, best click on them all while I jog my memory. Never get old, dear," Mags said with a heavy sigh.

Rachel peeled her jacket cuff back to check her watch and looked over at the superintendent's closed office door. Through the parted window blinds she could see Jenkins leaning back in his office chair having a heated conversation on the telephone. *I'm on a clock here, Mags,* she thought.

"Anyway, enough about me. What about you?" Mags asked, clicking on her fifth incorrect folder.

Rachel cast her glance back to her. "What about me?" she said, a little too brusquely.

Mags smiled but continued to stare down her nose at the screen. "You married? Single? Lesbian?"

Rachel let out a laugh. "Straight in there, eh?"

"That's me. Direct. Haven't got enough miles left on the clock to fanny about."

"I noticed. The former, I mean. You're not that old."

Mags looked up at Rachel in mock scorn. A slight smile formed at the corner of Rachel's lips. "Touché," she said, relaxing her eyes and grinning. "We'll get on, me and you. I can sense it. So?"

"What?"

"You didn't answer my question."

"Oh, right. I'm…separated actually. But we're working it out, my *husband* and I."

Mags continued scrolling through the desktop. "Did he travel up with you?"

"No. He's back home. Anyway, I'm sure I'll be kept busy with all of these cases." *That is, if we ever find them,* she added internally as Mags clicked on one of the last folder options.

———

OUTSIDE THE HOTEL, Katie stood on the pavement and looked down at Charlotte, who was catching on her tongue the few droplets of rain in the air. "So, you be a good girl for Mummy. I hope I see you again sometime?" She looked at Jenny, then up at the darkening clouds hovering over them. "You know, I could give you a lift to the station? It's only a few minutes in the car." She looked down at Jenny's cumbersome luggage, not helped by the awkward wrapping of the bunch of flowers she'd given her.

"You don't have a car seat for Charlotte," Jenny replied in a flat voice. "So… Bye then."

They stood facing each other, both not knowing how to part. Charlotte looked up at her mother, then at Katie.

"Bye," Katie replied, her voice barely above a whisper.

Jenny clasped her daughter's hand tighter and slung her handbag over her shoulder. Katie tugged her panda Trunki behind her while Jenny pulled her wheeled case with her free hand, the flowers poked stems-first into the open front pocket.

Katie watched them walk away. Then, when they were about ten feet away and about to cross the road, she called out, "Who's Mollie?"

Jenny stopped dead in her tracks, yanking Charlotte, who had carried on walking, backwards. She turned to face her sister. "What?"

"Mollie. When I was in the loo I heard you talking to Charlotte, after she found a photo in your phone case. So? Who is she?"

Jenny strode towards Katie, her expression stony. "Now is definitely *not* the time, Katie. We have a long journey." She looked down at Charlotte who was waving to a dog she'd seen across the road. "We've got to go."

"Why can't you tell me?" She looked down also at Charlotte. "What's so secret?" Then a thought crossed her mind and her tone softened. "Oh, Jen. Did you lose a child?" she added in a whisper.

"No, I did not," Jenny snapped. "Look, this is a hard enough time as it is, with Aunt Joan passing away. We'll discuss it another time. I need to go. Now."

Katie huffed. "But when, Jenny? We hardly see each other. In the next five years? Ten years? You're always fobbing me off. I just want a relationship with my sister. Is that so bad?"

"Look, I don't know when, OK?" Jenny growled. "I'll call you when we get home."

Katie watched, half angry, half sad, as Jenny and Charlotte walked across the road and disappeared around the corner, just as the storm clouds above her burst.

Chapter 5

RACHEL LEANED BACK on her white leather sofa and ran a hand through her long, dark hair. Curled up in her lap in a deep sleep was her black and white cat, Pickles, full and snoring after devouring the last of his dinner. Outside the streetlights glared through the gap in the green lounge curtains and every now and again a car swooshed past the terraced house she was renting. She reached forward and picked up the glass that was sat on her oak coffee table, took a swig of her orange juice and answered her ringing mobile.

"Bet your partner at work is shit," a sarcastic voice sounded through the phone. Michelle Barlow's Cornish lilt was unmistakeable to Rachel, making her laugh.

"Hello to you too, Shell. How's it going down there, *DC Barlow*?"

"Oohh, say that again, it sounds really sexy," Michelle replied.

"Stop it, you. I'm still your superior," Rachel chided, then softened her voice. "It's good to hear from you, mate. I miss you." She ran a hand over Pickles' short hair, causing him to purr.

"Miss you too. There's nothing else down here for you to

miss, though. Bore city now you've cleaned up the place. So, this new sidekick then? Tell me what she's like."

Rachel blew her cheeks out. "Well, you could say I've definitely drawn the short straw. Oh, Mags seems lovely enough, and everyone seems to like her. But her work ethic is not as, let's say, diligent as yours, Shell. I've got to get my teeth into an actual case soon, not an out of date case file, or what's the point me being up here?"

"Oh, sorry to hear that. Genuinely. I know how a good team around you matters. And you were the best around here. Like, not even joking, mate, you've got proper legend status around here. Even old hatchet-faced Hargreaves thinks the sun shines out of your arse. I think she was thinking of putting a plaque above your old desk when you left."

"Piss off. As if," Rachel said, laughing. "I'm sure the endless dinners with local councillors, bragging about how she's cleaned up the town, will suffice."

"So, does this 'Mags' bring in Krispy Kremes on a Friday then? I bet she don't."

"No, she barely brings her brain in most days. Today she spent about half an hour trying to remember her password to log on. I'll be at the end of my secondment up here, and her retiring, before we do any actual policing."

"Well, you can only do your best. Which I'm sure will be more than enough. And if you need an extra pair of eyes and ears, you know I'm always here for you, don't you?"

"Thanks, Shell. I really appreciate that. And I might take you up on that offer before long. Listen, I'd better go. My mum's trying to get through. But I'll ring you soon, OK? You take care."

"You too," Michelle replied before hanging up the phone.

Seconds later, Rachel's phone rang again. "Hi Mum. You OK?"

"I'm very well, thank you, darling. How are you doing up there? I hope they aren't keeping you too busy?" Rachel's mum said with the same note of concern in her voice that Rachel had come to expect, and accept.

"Well, I do have a certain amount of work to get done in the time they are paying me to be up here, so I need to make a good impression. You know this job isn't a nine-to-five thing, Mum." Rachel sighed. She was sick of having the same conversation with her mum day after day, week after week.

"Just as long as you promise me you won't do those all-nighters again. Not sleeping properly isn't good for your skin. And don't let Pickles out the front door yet. He won't know where he is for a while. Let him out in the back garden first for a few days. Are you eating properly?"

"Mum, of course I am," Rachel replied, guiltily remembering the Indian takeaway she'd ordered twenty minutes earlier.

"Have you heard from Adam?"

Rachel felt her heart drop. "He's seen my messages, but nothing yet. It may take some time for him to decide what he wants."

"He's hurting too, from what happened. You both need to get together and talk this through. Don't you think you've apologised enough? And you've changed your lifestyle now. Eased off a bit."

"I know, Mum. But he needs to find his own way back to me. I can't rush him."

The doorbell rang. "Mum, I've got to go. I'll speak to you at the weekend, OK?"

———

KATIE TURNED over in bed for the fourth time, and punched her pillow. Tom lifted his head and looked over to her through the half-light in their bedroom.

"Can't sleep?"

"Just feel churned up. After seeing my sister today, and the way she was acting. I'm all over the place."

Tom lifted his arm and cuddled into the back of Katie. "But it was nice to see your niece, though, wasn't it? I saw you with her at the funeral. You're a natural."

"Not that Jenny sees it that way. I kept asking her if I could see Charlotte again some time. I'd even drive up to Liverpool to see her, but it was still met with hostility."

"Give it time. She's probably just worried in case Charlotte gets attached to you and then you can't visit as often as you'd want."

Katie paused before answering. "Maybe? But I think she's keeping something secret."

"Like what?"

"I'm not sure. But I'm going to try and find out."

Tom nuzzled his mouth into her ear. "Well, seeing as though both of us are awake, why don't we try and…make our own babies?" He kissed her neck and moved his body on top of her. Katie lifted her arms over his head and stroked his neck. Despite the glint in his clear green eyes, she could only muster up a sad smile.

"Why hasn't it happened for us yet?"

"I don't know," Tom replied. "You've had a lot on your plate recently, with organising things for your aunt, and stress at work. You keep saying everyone there thinks Ofsted are due a visit so people are panicking. We just have to take the pressure off trying to rush it. It will happen, though, I know it. Two people who love each other as much as we do just can't not have children to share that love."

———

"Morning, Rachel," Supt. Jenkins said as he leaned around her open office door, a smile draped over his long, deeply lined face. "We've got a meeting in five with the boss, OK?"

"I'll be right there," Rachel replied, shuffling her papers into a folder and putting it in her letter tray. Grabbing her jacket from the back of the chair, she headed out towards Jenkins' office.

"Come in," Jenkins called back after Rachel knocked on the glass window of his office door. "Ah, Rachel, yes. Come in," he said as Rachel peered around his door. Standing next to his desk looking out of the window onto the carpark below was a tall, dark-skinned, middle-aged man. Powerfully built, he was dressed in a similar police uniform to Jenkins. Though, instead of the crown of a superintendent, his epaulettes featured a shiny pair of crossed tipstaves within a wreath.

The man by the window had a calm, collected stance about him. He turned and looked at Rachel, his dark brown face unreadable. "Allow me to introduce Assistant Chief Constable Richard Clifford," Jenkins said.

ACC Clifford walked around from behind the desk and held out a broad hand to Rachel, who shook it. His grip was tight, authoritative. His dark brown eyes were keen as they bored into her, trying to read her. His thick lips broke into a wide smile revealing perfectly white teeth. "Excellent to finally meet you, DI Morrison," he said, with a slight Jamaican lilt in his voice. "I've heard nothing but great things about you. Please, sit." He held out a hand to indicate the vacant chair by Jenkins' desk. After she'd sat down, so did the other two men. "I've set aside a budget to fund a small Task Force whose job it will be to conduct an urgent review into this division's handling of Missing Persons enquiries. The Task Force will be headed by you, DI Morrison. I've deemed this action neces-sary because a recent review of departmental performance highlighted that there were a disproportionate number of outstanding enquiries here compared to other divisions within the Force." His bushy black eyebrows lifted and lowered. "You got the job because I decided I wanted the best officer I could find to lead the Task Force. I asked Superintendent Jenkins to seek out a suitable candidate for me. He was at a dinner with your old boss, Superintendent Elaine Hargreaves down in

London last month, and got to talking about her most highly regarded officers. Your name came up."

Rachel's brow creased. "Really?" *Hargreaves hated me,* she thought. "I'm flattered that she would think so highly of me to mention *me.*"

"That's not all she did. She said you were the best detective she had. That she saw great things in the future for you."

Bloody hell, Rachel thought. *She must have been drunk.*

"So, after a phone call update from Graham here, I asked him to second you up from Cornwall, with Hargreaves' permission, that is. She agreed, as long as it was after you'd tied up all the loose ends with the Walker case. Seemed quite reluctant to let you go, but agreed it would be a nice change of scene for you."

"I'm honoured, sir," Rachel replied, looking at Jenkins, who let a smile twitch at the corners of his tight mouth.

"Now, the money won't last forever," ACC Clifford continued, clasping his hairy-backed hands together in front of him. "But I'm hopeful that in the short amount of time we have allotted to this project, you'll be able to bring this division's statistics in line with the others in the Force. The newly elected Mayor for Liverpool and the local council are on board and have made it part of their campaign to make a real drive to boxing off unresolved misper enquiries. Our mission is to spread more confidence in our community, especially as the council tax has recently gone up. We need the public on side. We need to impress."

ACC Clifford punctuated his last two statements with the finger point of an experienced politician. Supt. Jenkins folded his arms and sat back in his chair. Inwardly Rachel raised an eyebrow. She had wondered how long it would take until the ACC started spurting out managerial speak and doing political point scoring. Not long at all, it seemed.

"Well, I will do my very best, sir. You have my assurances on that." Rachel looked between Clifford and Jenkins with a smile of confidence on her face.

Clifford relaxed his broad shoulders and swapped nods with Jenkins. "I'm sure you will. I understand that you have been assigned an assistant? Graham, is that right?"

"Yes, I've assigned DC Maggie Chapman, one of our most experienced officers. Knows the city like the back of her hand. She can get us in all the back ways, if you know what I mean? My newly appointed DC, Chloe Sharp, will also be on the team, as I'm lining her up as Mags' replacement. And DC Johnny Bradley is on hand to assist with local knowledge also. He's my 'man about town'."

ACC Clifford squinted an eye and nodded. "Excellent. Well, with a crack team like this, how can we fail?" He spread his hands and grinned.

Rachel forced a smile back.

Chapter 6

KATIE TOOK another sip from her wine glass, as the conversation flowed all around her in the busy bar in Kemptown. Waitresses were carrying around large serving platters laden with martinis and bar snacks, and behind the bar mixologists were tossing and spinning silver cocktail mixers to the 'ooohs' and 'ahhhs' of the watching crowd. Three of Katie's friends from the nursery where she worked on her college placement, including her best friend—and line manager—Dawn, sat with her at a high bar table, mulling over the day, swapping stories about the individual disasters they'd had with their children, most including spillages or toilet incidents. Careful to laugh in all the right places, Katie paid just about enough attention to avoid too many concerned glances. After staring at her phone for a minute too long, Dawn noticed she'd gone quiet and turned away from the conversation, leaving the other two to carry on chatting.

"You OK, mate?" Dawn asked.

Katie looked up from her phone to meet Dawn's gentle blue eyes. "I'm fine. Just trying to write a text message to my sister. Trying to find the right words, you know?" She reached out and took a huge slurp from her white wine glass.

Dawn flashed a sympathetic smile. "I guess you're both

still grieving your aunt? It has only been a week or so since the funeral, so it's bound to be a bit raw still for you both." She swept a lock of long blonde hair from her face. "You don't really talk about her that much. Maybe this is an opportunity to reconnect?" Her words were interrupted by a loud beep from Katie's phone. Katie looked down at the message and frowned. Dawn noticed and put a hand on Katie's shoulder. "You don't really talk about your childhood, or when you used to live with Jenny up north. Where was it again?"

"Um… Sorry, I need to go." Katie dropped her phone into her jacket pocket and leaned down from her bar stool to pick her bag up off the floor, knocking into the table and rattling the wine glasses into each other. Dawn leapt into action to save her glass from spilling over.

"Oh, right. OK. You want me to walk with you? I don't mind," Dawn said, reaching down for her handbag, but when she looked up Katie had already left.

———

"You're home early," Tom said over his shoulder as he heard the front door slam and the interior door to the lounge open. He turned backwards to look at Katie from the cream leather sofa. "Good night with the girls?"

"I *finally* got a reply from Jenny," Katie replied, her face stained with dry tears and mascara streaks.

Tom leapt over the arm of the couch and rushed over to embrace her. "And?" he said, his green eyes wide.

"She said no. I gave her four possible dates for me to come up and see her, take Charlotte out for a milkshake or something, and she said no to all of them." Katie spread her hands. "I can't believe she's being like this."

"She said no?" Tom said, shaking his head. "I don't get it either. What's the story with you two? Christ, it's like she's holding something terrible against you, or something."

"Well, it wasn't a 'no', just an 'it's not a good time' sort of answer. But she's just fobbing me off, like usual. I mean, I've given her so much notice. But apparently all the dates are when she's got something on that can't be changed."

Tom sighed and gathered her up in his strong arms. He kissed the top of her head. "I'm sure she'll see sense soon. It'll just take time to build your relationship up again. Just keep on at her. I know how persuasive you can be. She'll come round in the end."

Katie lifted her wet face from his grey Metallica t-shirt. "What if she doesn't, Tom? What if I'm not even able to be an auntie, let alone a mum?"

———

"Morning, everyone. How are we getting on?" Rachel said, slinging her jacket over the back of the chair. All around the small table in her office, her officers had a blue cardboard folder each in front of them, ready to give her an update. Mags and Bradley were in attendance, along with two other detectives Rachel hadn't been formally introduced to yet. They sat next to each other across the other side of the table from Mags and Bradley, arms folded and eyes watchful. "Bradley, did you go round to the Connolly residence to check Hazel is alive and well, and not had her credit card cloned?" Rachel asked, looking over at the young detective, who was dressed as immaculately as usual in a grey three-piece suit with a navy-blue tie.

"Yes, boss, all sorted," Bradley replied. "I checked her date of birth with her, and the photo we had of her checks out. She was mystified that we were still looking for her, given that her husband rang control to cancel the misper report on the database as soon as she returned home the next day. Told me she only disappeared down to Harrods because she was picking up a surprise for his birthday. Didn't tell her husband for obvious reasons. She couldn't believe the hoo-ha it caused."

Rachel cast half an eye at Mags, who looked up at her

from her compact and pressed her lips together after reapplying her bright red lipstick. "Good. That's one case all boxed off. Great start, Bradley. Right, what else have you got?"

"I found this one right at the bottom of the pile. Once I read it I thought it would be good to start with, as there's a time press." He took out a piece of paper from his blue folder and slid it across the desk to Rachel. Seeing that all four chairs were already taken, Rachel slid her leather office chair over to the table, took out her reading glasses and pored over the piece of paper.

"Callum Davies. Thirty-two. Left behind a pregnant girlfriend. Nobody's seen or heard from him since," Rachel read out loud. She looked up at Bradley, then at Mags and slipped off her glasses. "Over a year ago now."

"That one stood out to me. His baby would be born now. Can't be easy for his missus, coping on her own. But it's up to you, boss. There are a couple of others that Mags found."

Mags put the compact away and opened her thin file. "Missing prostitute. Vanished eight years ago." She licked her finger and leafed through another blue folder. "Or a druggie vanished three years ago after a drop. Take your pick of those two."

"Missing after a drop?" Rachel repeated, raising an eyebrow. "How is that unsolved? Sounds pretty cut and dried to me." She cast a look around the table at the other DCs, who sniggered.

"This station is full of lazy bastards, and some pretty boys who don't like getting their hands dirty," a white-haired, grizzled detective chimed in, after folding his arms and looking directly at Bradley.

"Fur coat, no knickers, some," the black-haired, middle-aged DC sat next to him whispered, just loudly enough for Bradley to hear.

Rachel noticed Bradley's confident aura evaporate. He was now slumped in his seat looking down at the table and picked at the edge of it, his cheeks pink with embarrassment. Rachel flashed the two older DCs her sharpest stare. "I don't think we've been formally introduced. I'm Detective Inspector Rachel Morrison. And you two are?" she added.

The two DCs withered. The black-haired detective sat forward as the other man shifted in his chair. "DC Alan Palmer. This here is DC Colin Andrews," Palmer said. "We're here to assist while you get to know the place."

"Really? Well, I'm sure I'll do just fine with DC Chapman and DC Bradley, here. So, I think I'll have you two down in the archive room *assisting* me by sending up any records we need to take a look at and refiling the completed case files. Off you pop." She raised her eyebrows and nodded towards the door. Grumbling to each other, the two DCs lifted their bulk out of their chairs and sauntered off. "Well, now. Let's get on with it." Rachel looked at Bradley, whose eyes brightened as he straightened his back. "I think we'll start with the young lad that's missing. Callum Davies. Let's get him home to his baby, shall we?"

"I'll make some calls, arrange to visit his father down at the docks to go over his statement," Bradley said, reinvigorated.

As their eyes lowered to their work, a knock at the door came. Around it appeared Supt. Jenkins.

"Sorry to interrupt your train of thought, but I've asked DC Chloe Sharp here to join the team. She'll be taking over from DC Chapman in due course so it'll be good for her to muck in and get to know everyone."

The door opened to reveal a young smart-suited woman, in her late twenties, with asymmetrically bobbed blonde hair and keen blue eyes. She flashed a broad white smile, illuminating her attractive face even more.

Rachel stood up and walked around the desk. "Good to have you on board, DC Sharp. Take a seat. Do you know everybody?"

"I know Mags…sorry, I mean DC Chapman," Sharp said, biting her lip.

Mags laughed and swatted the air. "Oh, Chloe, don't be daft. You know it's Mags to you, babes. We're the same rank now you've passed your exam."

Chloe blew her cheeks out, causing her light fringe to ripple. "I know, but I should be more careful when meeting the bosses," she said out of the corner of her mouth.

Rachel nodded. "OK, well, welcome to the team, DC Sharp. This is DC Johnny Bradley and I'm…"

"You're Detective Inspector Rachel Morrison," Chloe interrupted, grinning with wide eyes like a ten-year-old meeting Harry Styles. "I've heard all about you. It's an honour working with you, ma'am." She bowed her head and looked as if she was about to curtsey.

Rachel held her hands up. "Relax, I'm not the Queen. Take a seat next to Bradley and let's get cracking."

Chloe did as she was told, her gawky gaze not dropping from Rachel, despite Bradley preening himself and straightening his jacket as the gorgeous figure of Chloe Sharp plonked herself next to him.

"I can't wait," Chloe gushed. "Missing persons cases have always interested me." She reached into her jacket pocket and took out her notebook. Her pen was poised, ready to take down every word Rachel spoke.

ACC CLIFFORD STOOD at the mirror in his opulent bathroom staring at his weary face. After dropping his toothbrush into its holder on the cream-coloured porcelain sink, he dried his hands on a fluffy white towel and walked into his spacious, immaculately decorated bedroom.

"Everything OK, dear? You look like you're in another world," his wife said. She was in her early fifties, her dark brown skin clear and radiant despite the lack of makeup. She wore a blush pink satin nightgown and was sitting up in bed with a huge burgundy-coloured damask-covered pillow propping her up. She placed her book face down on her lap with a well-manicured hand and awaited his reply.

"All good. My new DI has just started. She seems OK. A breath of fresh air, actually."

"Well then, that's good, isn't it? That police station needs some new blood and fresh thinking to flush out the stagnant air." She laughed at her extension of her husband's metaphor. "It'll be fine. Anyway, come to bed."

Clifford smiled and climbed into bed. He leaned over to kiss his wife on the forehead. "Night, darling."

———

RACHEL'S small living room was shrouded in darkness, with only a beam of moonlight illuminating the bottle of Chardonnay that sat on her coffee table. The one glass she'd poured out of it sat untouched next to it.

`Can we at least talk? Please? I'm so sorry. I miss you.`

She stared at the phone screen after typing out her message to Adam, hoping to see the two grey ticks turn blue. After a minute they did, but five minutes later, she threw her phone down on the white leather sofa next to her, realising for the thousandth time that a reply wasn't going to come. Leaning forward, she thought for one last second about not doing what she was about to do, but reached for the glass anyway. Necking the liquid in three gulps, she lay back on the sofa and pressed her face into a cushion, the blue fabric turning darker and darker as Rachel's tears soaked into it.

Chapter 7

"Morning, boss," a light voice chirped behind Rachel as she clinked the combination lock around the front wheel of her bike. She turned around to see Chloe Sharp beaming at her.

"Morning, Sharp. You rode in as well?" Rachel looked down at Chloe's blue Raleigh mountain bike.

"Yeah, I only live a few streets away, and you know what the parking's like over there." Chloe inclined her head to the Merseyside Police Headquarters car park. "Plus it keeps me fit. I like feeling the blood pump through me. Makes me feel alive, you know?" A cool morning breeze blew in off the Mersey which Chloe breathed in deep. "Best time of the day, this, don't you think?"

"You always in this early?" Rachel asked, looking at her watch.

"Yeah, I like getting an early start. Especially with the mornings so bright this time of year. You an early bird too then?"

"I like the quiet. Helps me get my thoughts together," Rachel added with a smile. She watched as Chloe fiddled with the awkwardly small key in her bike lock.

"I'm the same. No husband or kids to get ready for school. How about you?" Chloe lifted her face, triumphant that she'd finally clinked the lock into place around her bike chain. "Oh, sorry, boss. That's so none of my business." Her face reddened, even more than the exertion from securing her bike had caused.

"No, it's OK," Rachel replied, a little on the back foot from Chloe's personal question. Her keen blue eyes and open, pleasant face made it hard, though, for Rachel to reprimand her for her forwardness to a senior officer. "And no. Just my cat. No kids. Yet. But my husband and I… Well, it's complicated. Anyway, shall we go in? Otherwise our intentions of an early start seem a waste, don't you think?"

Chloe apologised again, but Rachel waved her hand to dismiss it.

"How are you finding working with Mags?" Chloe said as they walked up the concrete steps and through the entrance of the building.

"She's…interesting," Rachel replied with a glint in her eyes as they headed over towards the lifts.

"You mean she's a pain in the arse," Chloe whispered after leaning in a bit to Rachel. "She has a reputation around here as a bit of a dinosaur, but she's always been kind to me. Plus, she's a good copper. When I first started at this nick five years ago, she really took me under her wing."

"I do get the sense she's got a lot of useful qualities. She's a font of local knowledge for one thing, isn't she? She did well boxing off the Oswald case last week. You all did, actually." Rachel had been speaking into the air, but then turned to face Chloe and locked eyes with her. "I'm really glad to have you on the team, Sharp. We're making great headway with these misper cases."

Chloe grinned, the blood rushing to her cheeks. "Thank you. Same. We know you don't like to mess about. You like things sorted. We need that around here." She swallowed and looked away as Rachel punched the button for the floor they wanted.

"Well, thank you for saying. I don't want you all thinking

I'm the new broom, coming in to show you all how to do your job properly," Rachel said, her tone magnanimous even though she knew that was exactly the reason Jenkins had headhunted her. But young Chloe Sharp didn't need that hit to her confidence. Rachel could sense a good, diligent detective in her. "The Oswald case was a team effort. I saw how you all worked on it, so onwards to the next one, eh?"

"Definitely. I, for one, really want to get the Callum Davies case sewn up as soon as we can." Chloe set her face hard.

"Loving the determination," Rachel said.

"Well, I was looking into the case file last night before I left work for the evening, and it appears that one of Callum's trainers was found in the undergrowth by the side of Canning Dock."

"Canning Dock? That's just across the road from here, isn't it?" Rachel interjected.

"Yeah, just a few minutes' walk away. It's as if he wanted us to find it. What I don't understand is that, apart from getting a positive ID on it by his father, it was kind of forgotten about by the investigating officers at the time. I mean, I know I'm still wet behind the ears, but I would have thought that would trigger more of an investigation, wouldn't it?" Chloe shook her head as she thought about it.

"The department must have been overworked and under-staffed back then, I guess. ACC Clifford's been here for years and has only recently been given more funding due to growing public pressure on him to get results, hence why you're here assisting us, so now we can take a closer look at these cases," Rachel surmised. "What else did you pick up on from the notes?"

Chloe licked her full, red lips, her eyes wide and focused intently on Rachel's watchful stare. "Well, Callum worked for his dad in a car garage near Princes Dock, a bit further up from Canning Dock. But his dad was said to be really strict with him. He sounds a bit of a shit, actually, if you read between the lines of the statement he made after Callum disappeared. He sounded really miffed. Said Callum had 'dropped him right in it'. I got the sense that Callum was planning to leave his dad's business to get a better paid job to support his girlfriend, now he was about to become a father himself."

"Conclusion?" Rachel said.

"Maybe his dad killed him? Angry that Callum was leaving him and betraying him? He works on the docks so it wouldn't be too hard to dump a body? Or, maybe it was suicide? Maybe Callum felt he was trapped?"

Rachel looked over at Chloe and narrowed her eyes. "Why don't we sit together this morning and go over Mr. Davies senior's statement? You've an eye for detail that I think could be really important," Rachel added just as Chloe's face lit up. "I've already decided to take Mags with me when I pay Callum's girlfriend a visit to get some more background on the circumstances before he disappeared, but I've got Bradley going over to speak to Mr. Davies this afternoon. I think I'll let you go with him and see what you both can turn up. Reckon you can deal with the charming sounding Mr. Davies senior?"

"Sleeves rolled up and ready to go," Chloe replied.

———

"This is the place," DC Johnny Bradley said as he turned the car off the main road by Princes Dock and onto the gravel outside a dingy, run down car garage. Car parts littered the area, and several hollow, rusting chassis lay in in disrepair all around. There was a huge tyre wall at the side of the garage, half-covered by a grimy blue tarpaulin. Overgrown weeds, green mould and splodges of bird droppings decorated the pile of tyres. As Bradley and Sharp surveyed the area for signs of life through the windscreen of their Ford Focus, two large white seagulls hovered above, squawking then diving for half a bacon sandwich that lay by the metal legs of an old, grease-stained blue garden chair.

"Yep, looks like it. See?" DC Chloe Sharp pointed up to the sign above the garage doors. "Barry Davies." She scrunched her nose up. "Given up on finding his son alive then, clearly."

Bradley followed her point and saw a black cross through the 'and son' part of the sign. "Nice chap. You ready?"

"Let's do this," Chloe replied, reaching onto the back seat for her grey suit jacket as Bradley straightened his purple tie and smoothed down his white shirt. They both exited the car and strode over to the open wooden doors of the garage. Bradley banged his fist against the door and called out. Moments later, a fat balding middle-aged man waddled over to them, ducking underneath the car lift on the way. He wiped his pudgy hands on an oil-stained rag.

"Can I help you, lad?" the man said with the trace of a snarl on his thick lips. When they got close, they saw he was heavily pockmarked and had greasy black thinning hair scraped back and protuberant cold blue eyes. All down his dirty blue overalls were stains of oil and grease.

"Barry Davies?" Bradley asked.

"Who wants to know?" the man replied. His eyes drifted over Chloe's slim, suited figure, from boots to brow, before returning to Bradley who was stern-faced awaiting his reply. "Yeah, I'm Barry Davies. Is this about that BMW that came in last week?"

Bradley held his hand up. "No, Mr. Davies. It's about your son. Callum?"

Davies' face darkened. "Not interested. Now, if you don't mind? I'm a busy man." He turned to walk away.

"He's been gone a year now, Mr. Davies. His shoe was left by Canning Dock. You identified it at the time as belonging to him, right? Are you not in the least bit worried about him?" Chloe said. Bradley held his arm out to stop her following Davies back into his garage.

"Easy, Sharp. We want answers, not to piss him off," Bradley said. But her words had angered Davies into turning back around and walking straight up to her. His eyes were like fire.

"Now, you listen to me, love. That little shit fucked off last year and left me here in the lurch running this place. Got his bird up the duff and panicked most likely, thinking he had to grow up finally. Said before he went that he was depressed and couldn't handle life anymore. Never even thought that *I* might have problems of my own to deal with. He's probably at the bottom of Canning Dock, and could be for all I care. He always was a waste of space, that lad. Wasn't my fault his mother died when he was two. I did my best for the boy. If you find him, tell him he's dead to me. Now, fuck off, the pair of you."

———

IN THE GLORIOUS May evening sunshine, Katie looked out on to the English Channel and held the small brown urn close to her chest. Feeling the sharp grey pebbles on Brighton beach dig into her sandaled feet, she breathed in a huge lungful of sea air and steadied herself as the cold water lapped at her toes. Tom walked up behind her and laid a hand on her shoulder.

"Doris and Violet are here now. Dawn's just locking her car and heading down the boardwalk. How are you holding up?" he said in a soft voice. Katie looked into his clear green eyes, moist with unfallen tears.

"I think I'm ready." She looked over his shoulder and saw the two older ladies from the funeral, both of them decked out in summer dresses and light macs, each a different pastel shade. Doris waved a handkerchief-laden hand, then dabbed her eyes. Approaching behind them was the rushing figure of Dawn.

"Sorry I'm late, Katie," Dawn called over. "Are we ready to start?"

Tom looked at Katie, who nodded. The group approached and Katie took out a piece of paper and began reading.

"Auntie Joan loved the sea. She loved it here in Brighton. Lived here all her life. In that house over there." She inclined her head to the row of Victorian terraces bordering the quiet stretch of road just outside the main town centre. "Her last wishes were for me to scatter her ashes here. On this spot. Where her husband Sam, God rest his soul, proposed to her in 1981, at this exact time on her twenty-first birthday. Auntie Joan had a good life. When her sister-in-law, my mother, died twenty-two years ago now, I was only five." Katie stopped, realising how much time had passed since that day. She looked at the ripple of waves in the distance for a moment, then refocused and continued. "I was sent down here to live two years after. Auntie Joan never judged me. Never put too much pressure on me to fit in with life down here. I didn't settle straight away. But she gave me the time and understanding to become who I wanted to be in life. I just wish she could have lived to see me start my own family. See my children grow up. Sixty years old. Far too soon to be taken." Katie looked down at the urn and unscrewed the cap. "Auntie Joan, I will always remember you for your kindness, understanding, and you being a mum to me. I love you and I miss you so much. Goodbye." Katie waited for the small group to gather close behind her before taking two steps forward into the swell of the waves. Reaching down, she emptied the contents of the urn, watching as they mingled with the white foam and tiny thin strings of greeny-black seaweed. The wave carrying the ashes receded, washing away all trace of her auntie.

"She'll be looking down on you, proud as anything of you, Katie," Dawn said, walking up to hug her.

"I hope so."

"Any news on Jenny yet?" Dawn asked.

"Actually, you've just reminded me," Katie said. She handed Dawn the now-empty urn and fished into her jacket pocket, taking out her mobile phone. "Nothing." She heaved a huge sigh. Then, Katie began typing out a message.

"What are you putting?" Dawn asked.

"I'll tell you if I get anything back," Katie replied before clicking on send.

"We'd better get back. It'll be getting dark soon," Tom announced, looking down at their lengthening shadows.

"Goodbye, Auntie Joan. Thank you for everything," Katie whispered to the ocean before turning around and following the little group away.

When they returned home, Katie couldn't help but notice that Tom seemed agitated. He walked through the front door and into the kitchen, taking a bottle of beer out of the fridge. He snipped the cap off and slammed the bottle opener down on the counter.

""You OK, babe?" Katie asked from the kitchen doorway.

"What was all that about, you saying to Dawn, 'I'll tell you if I get anything back'? From who? About what?" He took a slurp of beer and glared at her.

"Jenny. I just want to delve a little deeper into something, that's all. Nothing sinister for you to worry about."

"Listen. If it's about this 'Mollie' business, maybe Jenny doesn't want you to know about it. You're not exactly close. If she doesn't want to talk to you about it then you should just accept it. We've got other things to be planning, not you sticking your oar in where it's clearly not wanted." His green eyes were cold and angry, for the first time Katie could remember seeing them this way. She slammed her keys down on the counter near the door.

"I don't know who I am anymore. Can't you understand that? I have no roots, no family and no sense of belonging here anymore. I came down here when I was so young. I can't even remember my life in Liverpool, let alone remember any friends I might have had. Have you any idea how that feels? I don't hear from my dad and don't have a mum. Fucking hell, Tom, I don't even share the same *accent* with Jenny, let alone anything else. And to top it all off, my own niece thinks I'm a total stranger. I just want answers from Jenny. Is that so bad? I just need something to anchor myself to."

"And you think your sister is it?" Tom replied through tight lips.

"I don't know. I just want to find out a bit more about where I grew up. About Jenny. And who this mysterious 'Mollie' is."

"She's been the one ignoring *you*, remember. Maybe she's not interested," Tom snapped

"She's grown up alone too. She might not have understood why Dad couldn't cope with the two of us. Maybe she feels guilty that she got to stay and I was sent away. I think she's just protecting herself."

"From what?"

"Our past."

Tom picked up his beer and nodded, his tongue pressing into his cheek. "Right, well, I guess if you have to do this then you will. I know better after five years together to try and talk you out of anything." He walked past her in the doorway and stopped just long enough to kiss her lightly on the cheek.

Chapter 8

RACHEL STRODE into the buzzing incident room, past the junior detectives who were writing case notes on whiteboards at either side of the room and the admin clerks filing their notes in cabinets beside them, and placed her takeaway coffee down on Mags' desk. "Have you managed to find the other statements from the Davies case?"

Mags looked up from her phone. "The which case?"

Rachel looked at Mags' phone screen and inwardly sighed when she saw her Facebook timeline full of holiday photographs. "The Callum Davies case? Young lad? New father? The case we're working on?" She spread her arms.

"Oh, bloody hell, yes. Of course. Right." She put her phone face down on the desk and scrabbled through the piles of paper cluttered up around her. "Um…leave it with me. It's on my list to organise these by lunchtime."

Rachel nodded and picked up her coffee. Three steps away from Mags' desk, she turned back. "Oh, and did you get a chance to contact that social worker we spoke about in yesterday's briefing?"

"She doesn't work there anymore. I tried her office and her mobile. Nothing."

"Where does she work now?"

"Oh, I forgot to ask. I just thought we had enough statements already from that agency, that hers wouldn't be that important."

"Mags, come on," Rachel said, sighing at length. "You've been in this game long enough to know *every* statement is important."

The young PC, Mick, walked over to Mags' desk, grinning broadly.

"How's my work mum this morning?" He reached around the desk to embrace Mags.

"Hiya Mick, my little honey bun. Still with that girly?"

Rachel looked to the heavens and turned to head into her office. Waiting for her at the door was Superintendent Jenkins, his arms folded, his watchful eyes narrowed.

"You've got Laurel and Hardy all wrapped up in one there, Morrison," he said, giving her a sardonic little smile.

Rachel forced a smile back.

"In all seriousness, she's a good copper, Mags. She cares. Never wanted to rise through the ranks, but that's only because she was always more of a team worker than a leader. Just make sure you tap into her experience. She's good at what she does." He turned to leave.

"With respect, sir, why was she assigned to me?" Rachel's question was politely put, but her tone was accusing.

"We thought you might work well together. That's why I brought in DC Sharp. Youth added to experience, all girls together, that kind of thing."

His laugh annoyed Rachel, but her professionalism reminded her to remain deferential. Jenkins seemed to have forgotten about her own extensive experience including her years in the Met down in London. Fuming, she left the office and headed into the ladies' toilet and began splashing her face with water from the sink.

"Oh, hello again," a timid voice piped up from the sink

next to Rachel's. Rachel lifted her wet face and reached for a paper towel. A plump woman of around fifty stood staring expectantly at her. She was about six inches shorter than Rachel, with long ginger hair that was slightly curly, and a pair of horn-rimmed glasses on a string around her neck. "Remember me? Tina Saunders. I work in admin. We met on your first day here. I sorted out your ID." Tina's hazel eyes fixed on Rachel, who finally placed her and nodded.

"Of course. Hi."

They stood in awkward silence for a few moments while Rachel dried her hands and reapplied her dark red lip gloss. Tina lingered by her side.

"Was there something I can help you with, Tina?" Rachel asked as she screwed the top back on her lip gloss and smacked her lips to spread the gloss out evenly.

"Well, yes, there was," Tina replied, scrunching her paper towel over in her pudgy, clenched hands. "I notice a lot around here. Have done for years. And you seem like a lovely girl. I saw that from the first day. I said to myself, 'Tina,' I said, 'you keep an eye on that girl. She doesn't know half of the things that go on here. The characters who work here. The lies.'"

Rachel held her hands up. "Tina, what is it? I need to get back to my desk." She spoke as gently as her rapidly waning patience could allow her to.

Tina's stare hardened, her voice more determined and focused now. "Watch your back here, Detective Inspector. Not everyone is as *friendly* as they seem."

Tina turned and left the ladies' toilet, with Rachel left in a weird mix of confusion and disbelief. *Have I just been warned?* she thought.

––––––

TOM SLOPED barefoot down the soft, white carpeted stairs rubbing the sleep out of his eyes. He yawned loudly as he entered the kitchen, stopping when he saw Katie sat at the oak breakfast bar nursing a half-drunk cup of coffee.

"You're up early," he said. He nodded down to her cup. "Want a refill?"

"No thanks. I'm not feeling too good, actually. I've called in sick."

"Called in sick?" Tom repeated. "You've never done that in the whole time you've worked there. What's wrong?"

"Not sure. Maybe I'm due on or something? You know when I'm stressed my cycle goes up the wall. It feels like a period pain, but without the period, if you know what I mean? Just feel hot and bothered."

Tom placed a palm on her forehead. "Maybe you should go back to bed then. You probably got cold at the beach last night. Want me to call in at the boatyard? I can stay home and look after you? Might even be some homemade soup in it for you?" He smiled and wrapped his arms around her neck. But Katie squirmed away.

"No, it's OK. I'll just go take a bath and get back into bed or something. Hot water bottle and some crap telly and I'll be fine. Plus, you've already taken too much time off. You can't lose that job, Tom."

"OK then. If that's what you want," he said in a quiet voice. "I'll go run you a bath."

He walked back upstairs and left Katie in the kitchen. Looking back, he noticed her scrolling through her phone and frowning each time her thumb stopped moving.

The atmosphere inside Rachel's office was one of pure concentration. Heads were down, analysing old police statements with a fine-toothed comb, gentle murmurs rippling around the rectangular table in the corner. Every now and again, eyes locked and nods followed. Mags had her glasses on the end of her nose as she pored over one statement in particular and made a few notes on her pad. Chloe and Rachel sat next to each other, looking down at a file and sharing their hypotheses. DC Bradley was in the other corner of the office speaking in hushed tones on his phone. Outside, Supt. Jenkins was peering into Rachel's office through the gap in the blinds, not noticing ACC Clifford walking quietly up behind him.

"How's my crack team getting on?" ACC Clifford said, his deep voice vibrating in Jenkins' ear.

"Great so far. A couple of cases already boxed off, and the next being worked on as we speak."

Clifford smiled and rocked back on his heels. "I had to twist some arms to get that funding. I don't want it wasted. You hear what I'm saying?" He gave Jenkins a sharp look.

"Loud and clear, sir," Jenkins replied.

"Results, Graham. That's what we all want. We're on a time press, remember."

Jenkins flashed Clifford a confused look. "But what about any cases that don't get solved in time?"

"Those ones will have to remain unsolved. Or better yet, buried."

"The IPCC would never let us get away with that. Not to mention the press, and the families of those mispers," Jenkins said, shaking his head.

"I know. It will look much better for us all if *all* of those unsolved cases get put to bed once and for all. One way or another. Otherwise it's not just my arse on the line, it's yours too."

———

Lying back on her couch, Katie pulled her blue bathrobe tightly around her. An hour in a hot bubble bath had relaxed her only to a point, but as she scrolled through her messages to Jenny, her hackles began to rise again. A text from Tom flashed up on the screen, breaking her concentration. After a quick text back to tell him she didn't need any painkillers picking up, she clicked back into the sent messages folder.

"What did I say wrong?" she asked herself as she read over the wording of all her messages. Her thumb hovered over the Facebook app on her phone. She tapped it and scrolled through Jenny's timeline. "Active one fucking hour ago?" she raged at the screen. "Right, plan B then." She scrolled through Jenny's list of friends and clicked on the top picture, the woman Katie knew was Jenny's best friend. "Right, 'Hayley Whittaker', let's see what you're about then." To her surprise, Jenny appeared in this woman's profile picture, pouting at the camera as if they didn't have a care in the world. Seeing Hayley's privacy settings allowed strangers to private message her, Katie typed out a message and pressed send.

Hi Hayley, hope you're well? I know that you're my sister Jenny's closest friend and I was just a bit worried about her. She seemed to get upset the other day when I mentioned a 'Mollie'. Do you know anything about this girl?

Within a minute, Katie read Hayley's curt reply.

It's not my place to say. You need to speak to Jenny about this. Thanks.

"What the fuck?" Katie said, her face frozen in disbelief, feeling more confused and in the dark than ever.

———

Jenny's yoga studio was a small, simply decorated room in a converted warehouse unit near the Albert Dock. Its white walls and soft marble effect linoleum flooring gave the room a calmness that befitted its purpose. The amber glow from the uplighters fixed to the walls radiated warmth and peace.

Jenny, barefoot and wearing purple Lycra leggings and a matching vest top, stood at the front of the small group that had arrived for their class and switched on the relaxation music. She smiled at them.

"Good morning, everyone. So today, we're going to start with some gentle stretching and—."

"Sorry we're late," two breathless voices sounded from the doorway. The two older ladies dropped their bags by the coat hooks and ripped their coats off, revealing their matching Lycra outfits. They took their shoes and socks off.

"That's OK, Jean. Why don't you and Flora just join at the back there," Jenny replied, pointing to an empty space behind the back row of the group. They did so, and, just as Jenny was about to press play on the docking station, her phone lit up with a notification. Gazing down at it, she saw it was from Hayley.

Your sister has been asking about Mollie. Don't worry, I didn't tell her anything. But just wanted to give you the heads-up.

"Um...Jen? Are we starting soon?" a dark-haired young woman from the front row said in a meek voice.

"Hmm?" Jenny muttered back. She looked up at the woman.

"Are you OK?" the woman asked.

"What? Yes. Right. Let's get started." Jenny threw her phone back down onto her gym bag and motioned for the woman to rejoin the front row. Seconds later, she paused. "Sophie, can you just start the warm-up?" she said to the dark-haired woman, her face turning grey. "I'll be back in a minute." She strode over to the ladies' toilets, then ran as the acid caught in her throat. She reached the cubicle just in time, before a plume of vomit erupted out of her and crashed against the inside of the toilet bowl.

———

"WELL, I think we've done enough work for one day," Rachel said to the bleary-eyed group beavering away at the paper and coffee cup-laden briefing table in the corner of her office. Sighs of relief rippled around the room. "Thanks for today, everyone." She stood up, removed her reading glasses and pinched the bridge of her nose.

"What's say we all go to the Baltic Market? First round's on me. Boss?" Mags packed her pens away and looked up at Rachel.

Rachel smiled and shook her head. "No, I can't. I'm going to stay here for a bit. Got things to do. But thanks. You all go and relax. You've earned it after today."

"Blimey, you're keen," Mags chuckled as she slid on her beige trench coat and tied the belt in a bow.

"I'm on a timer, aren't I?" Rachel riposted with a grin.

"OK, well, enjoy. Johnny, Chloe, let's go." Mags rounded them up and headed towards the door.

Bradley grabbed his coat from the hook and slung an arm around Mags. "So I guess if you're getting the bevvies in, I'm on crisp duty again?"

"Yep. You know it." Mags grinned. "But no pork scratchings again. They played havoc with my bowels last time." Bradley grimaced at the image and then laughed as they walked out together.

Rachel piled up the folders from the table, not noticing one person was left in her office until she stood up straight. "You not going with them, Sharp?"

Chloe half smiled. "No. Not really feeling it tonight. Well, the Baltic, that is. I could stay and help you out here, if you like?"

Rachel laughed. "Haven't you got better things to go home to? You don't want to be stuck here all night with me and these things." She waved the folders in the air.

"No. Nothing better to go home to. I'd like to help crack on with these cases," Chloe replied. She swept a strand of blonde hair from her brow.

"OK then. We can start on this one." Rachel passed her a folder from the top of her pile. "The statement from Callum Davies' girlfriend regarding the night he disappeared. I'm seeing her tomorrow so I need to get my facts straight." She walked over to her desk and fished into the pocket of her jacket which was wrapped around the chair. "Here, why don't we order in? It could be a long one." She took a credit card out of her purse and handed it to Chloe.

"Sure. What's your favourite?"

"Chinese. Sweet and sour chicken."

"Same," Chloe said in a quiet voice as Rachel sat back down at the table to spread the files out again.

"And get some chips, too. I'm starving."

———

Jenny sat on her living room couch nursing a tepid bowl of chicken and rice. She was still wearing her yoga clothes and her blonde hair was messy from her class. She stirred her fork around the bowl while staring into space, her blue eyes vacant.

"Is it not very nice?" her boyfriend asked. He gazed at her with soft brown eyes, concern etched on his handsome features.

"Hmm? No, it's lovely. Thank you. I'm just not that hungry." Jenny replied, refocusing her eyes on the TV programme they were watching. She lifted a forkful of chicken to her mouth and chewed slowly.

"Oh, that reminds me," Sam said through a mouthful of rice. "Your sister tried calling me twice today. I was driving the cab so I couldn't answer, but she left me a voicemail." He reached over to the black glass-topped coffee table in front of them and picked up his phone.

Jenny stopped chewing. "What did it say?"

"I'll play it for you now."

The message blared out. 'Hi Sam, it's Katie. I was

wondering if you could pass on a message. Um…could you please ask Jenny to call me urgently? It's important.'

"She sounds in a right state. What's going on?" Sam asked when the message ended.

"Nothing. Don't worry about it." She pointed her bowl at him. "This is lovely, by the way. Thank you."

———

Rachel returned home at the end of what had felt like an extraordinarily long day. She closed her front door and dropped her keys in a small wooden bowl on the hall table. Stacked along the length of the narrow hallway were different sized brown cardboard boxes, yet to be unpacked. Even though she'd only been there a matter of weeks, Rachel didn't feel quite at home there yet, and hadn't decided where things should go. Even boxes with 'kitchen' labelled on them hadn't quite found their way in there yet.

She walked over and laid a hand on one box in particular and sighed as she read the label, 'Adam's stuff'. As she took her coat off and reached up to the hooks on the wall near the door, she felt a faint buzz from her mobile phone in her pocket. She took it out and read the message.

```
Really enjoyed our power hour this
evening. I'll type up our notes from the
statements we went through first thing in the
morning ready for your visit to Callum's
girlfriend. And thank you for the Chinese.
Such a nice change from eating alone at home.
See you in the morning, boss. Chloe x
```

Rachel closed her eyes after reading the message, wishing it had been from Adam. Quickly she tapped a few words of a response to Chloe and pressed send. Walking into the living room, she collapsed exhausted on the sofa and smiled. It felt nice to have at least one friend in this new city, even if it was someone a couple of ranks below her, and not the 'done thing' to fraternise with the underlings. But Chloe Sharp had an aura about her, one of excitement and spirit for the job and the chase of solving mysteries. Rachel remembered having that feeling once, many years ago. But now it was all about getting the job done, even if that meant that spirit had waned a bit over the last few years. Chloe Sharp could be the breath of fresh air she needed to start to enjoy the job again.

Chapter 9

"Ready to go?" Rachel said as she walked up to Mags' work desk.

"All set." Mags logged off her computer and stood up to put on her beige trench coat. She picked up her car keys and slipped her black spiral bound notebook into her pocket. "She was devastated when Callum disappeared, poor love. That baby will be almost seven months old by now. Shall I drive?"

The house they arrived at fifteen minutes later was a yellow-bricked mid-terraced house on a quiet street just off Smithdown Road, three miles from the city centre. Cars were parked on both sides of the narrow street, leaving just enough of a gap for Mags to manoeuvre her Audi along the grey, patchwork tarmac and park in a space in front of the house. Around the front window on the right side of the door was a halo of red-painted bricks and a black cable ran down from an old satellite dish fixed just above it. At the kerb of the cracked concreted path in front of the door there was a white plastic bin bag full of broken baby toys next to a row of six purple wheelie bins. Rachel stepped past them and approached the white PVC front door. She lifted the brass knocker and tapped on the door.

"Hello?" came a thin voice behind the door.

"Hi, is that Courtney? Courtney Wallace?" Rachel said.

"Who is it?"

"I'm Detective Inspector Rachel Morrison." Rachel fished into her pocket for her warrant card. "Can you open the door, please?"

The door opened a crack and a pale, tired face appeared. "I've just got the baby down. Is this about Callum? Have you found him?"

Rachel's face softened into a sympathetic smile. "Can we come in? I promise we'll be quiet."

Courtney glanced down at the warrant card Rachel was holding in her direction. She closed the door and removed the chain. "Come in," she said, opening the door. She was wearing an oversized white Beatles t-shirt and blue faded skinny jeans. Her long dark brown hair was tangled and flat on one side. She leaned down to move a bag of rubbish from behind the door to let them pass. "I'm sorry about the mess. I'm still working things out, you know?"

"Oh, don't worry about that, love. You should see my desk at work," Mags said with a motherly smile.

"Courtney, this is Detective Constable Chapman," Rachel said. "We haven't found Callum yet, but we are looking into his case right now. We just need to establish a few facts about the night Callum disappeared." She put her warrant card away and took out her notebook.

Courtney nodded and led them into a small living room to the right of the long hallway. It was sparsely furnished, with only a brown leather three-piece suite which looked like it had seen its fair share of charity shops, a pine sideboard and a matching coffee table. A small flat screen TV sat in the corner on a brown faux leather dining chair. Next to the larger of the couches was a cheap white-painted wooden crib with a baby asleep in it. Courtney wandered over to the crib and checked on the baby, tucking his arm back under his blanket.

"Can I get you both a tea?" Courtney asked.

Mags, catching a faint nod from Rachel, turned to Courtney and smiled. "Ooh, that'd be lovely. I'll give you a hand, shall I?" She followed Courtney out of the living room. Rachel put her notebook back in her jacket pocket and took the opportunity to have a look around the room. Nothing looked out of place or suspicious in any way. The simple home of a young twenty-something mother, complete with bag of dirty nappies at the side of the crib in the corner—the only part of the room Rachel had yet to inspect. She bit her lip and took a few steps closer to the crib, looking down into it. The baby was lying on his back wearing a white sleep suit with an elephant on it. He had sandy blond hair and features which reminded Rachel strongly of Callum's photograph on his case notes. After a few minutes of watching him in silence, Rachel reached a tentative hand down to the baby's pudgy little fist. Once her finger had slipped inside it, the baby gripped it. Rachel felt something inside her pang. She watched as the baby began to stir, then moments later he began to grizzle. "Shhh, there, there, little guy, it's OK. Shhh." The baby wriggled and began to cry. "Courtney? Your baby is waking up. Courtney?" But no one appeared at the living room door. With no other option as the baby's cries grew into heaving sobs, Rachel leaned down and picked him up, holding him almost at arm's length. "Shhhh. Come on, mate, it's OK. Shhhh." Rachel rocked him from side to side, her frustration and anguish growing as the baby continued to wriggle in her grasp. Mags appeared at the living room doorway and rushed over.

"Here, let me." She lifted the baby out of Rachel's arms and held him close to her chest. "Ooh, there, there, little man. What's all the fuss about, eh? Shhhh." As if by magic, the baby stopped crying and sniffed. He looked up at Mags through large inquisitive blue eyes.

"Is he alright?" Courtney said, appearing at the living

room doorway with a mug-laden tray. She rushed over to Mags and the baby.

"He's fine, love. Here, let me take that tray and you take the boy."

Seconds later, he was falling back to sleep in his mother's arms. Mags put the tray down on the coffee table.

"What's his name?" Rachel asked, wiping a strand of hair from her eyes.

"Tommy. He'll be seven months next week. He's just started teething so he's not sleeping that well." Courtney lowered Tommy back into the crib and stroked his face with her finger.

"Courtney, can you tell us about the night Callum disappeared?" Rachel asked.

"He'd been off with me for a few weeks before. Never said why."

"How did he feel about becoming a father?"

Courtney sat down on the couch. "He was dead excited when I told him. Couldn't wait. He found this place for us as soon as his universal credit came through. But then, about a week before he disappeared, he seemed really distracted. He'd been to see his dad a few nights earlier. We had tea on the night he disappeared but he hardly ate a thing. Then he put his trainers on and went out. It was about nine o'clock. I waited up all night but he never came home. I called the police later that day. No one got back to me. I didn't really know what to do. My parents pretty much disowned me when I got with Cal. So here we are. Me and Tommy. Just waiting. Waiting for Daddy to come home to us, aren't we, lad?" She looked into the crib at Tommy who was now sleeping soundly again.

"And he didn't say anything that would help us to understand why he left, or where he went that night?" Mags asked.

"No. Nothing." Courtney looked up at Rachel, her eyes moist. "Please find him. We need him home. Tommy needs his daddy. He'd be a great dad. And he has the most amazing son. Help us be a family. Please."

Rachel smiled with as much hope as she could muster. "We'll do our best. Thank you for your time, Courtney. We'll see ourselves out." She turned back at the living room doorway and gazed at the crib. "You take care of yourself. And that little one."

Chapter 10

RACHEL WALKED into her office on Monday morning and looked around it, feeling clearer headed after taking the time before the weekend to tidy and arrange it properly. On the desk her pens were all standing proudly in newly bought pen pots next to the computer, and her blue case folders were now labelled and stacked in date order from left to right on the shelves. Satisfied with the order she'd made of chaos, she sank down into her office chair and took a huge swig from her bottle of orange juice.

"You'll turn into that stuff if you're not careful," Mags said with a cheery grin as she pushed open the door and placed a folder on Rachel's desk.

"Vitamin C, Mags. Keeps the colds away," Rachel replied, smacking her lips and reaching for the file.

"Really? I'm always getting the sniffles, even in summer. I should take a leaf out of your book. So, did you do anything nice over the weekend?" Mags said, lingering by the door.

"Not really. Just got my house sorted finally. You?" Rachel pored over the folder without looking up.

"Oh yes. Me and Chip, that's my husband, went to The London Carriage Works for dinner Saturday night. The rib-eye steak and truffle mash is to die for."

70

Rachel's head snapped upwards. "The London Carriage Works? On a copper's wage?" She laughed.

"Chip paid, not me. I know. I'm a lucky girl. He knows how to keep me happy, does old Chip," Mags said with a wink. "He earns way more than me, and I am very much milking the hell out of that fact. He knows which side his bread's buttered anyway." Mags stroked her eyebrow with her little finger and gave Rachel a mock snooty look.

Rachel inwardly stifled a yawn. "I'm sure he does. Anyway, how are you getting on with those statements? Found any new leads?"

Mags held her hands up. "It's on my to-do list for today."

"Right," Rachel replied, fighting the urge to ask Mags in the most professional way she could why they hadn't already been done, over a week since she'd asked for them to be on her desk. "OK then. By the end of the day, though, OK?" She flashed Mags a pointed look.

"You have my word, boss," Mags replied, turning around and heading back out of the office to her cluttered desk. Rachel got up a few seconds later to look through the blinds at her. Sure enough, exactly as she expected, Mags sat down at her desk, ignored the files and had begun scrolling through her phone.

Looks like I'm going to have to put a rocket up your arse, DC Chapman, Rachel thought.

______

Tom slipped his key in the door and opened it, dropping his bag down by the shoe rack. With the sun outside setting, he switched on the hall light and recoiled, seeing Katie sat in silence staring up at him from her seated position at the bottom of the stairs.

"Christ, babe, you almost gave me a heart attack. What are you doing sitting down there?"

"I'm going up north, Tom. I'm going to visit the place in

Liverpool where I grew up. I need to find out what the hell is going on."

———

RACHEL LOOKED up at the clock on the wall in her office. After promising herself she wouldn't stay late that night, she sighed inwardly as the time read 7:30. Not ever staying a minute after 5:30, Mags had gone home, and in the large space outside Rachel's office, all cubicles appeared vacant. She looked back down at the folder she was reading through.

"Bloody social media," a deep, booming voice echoed through the incident room. Supt. Jenkins' tall, wiry frame appeared at Rachel's open door. "Everyone wants to know the ins and outs of a duck's arse these days. Can't let the police get on with their job. They've always got some smart-arse comment to post about the one thing in a million we're *not* doing."

Rachel looked up and slipped her reading glasses off her face. "Sir?"

"Oh, nothing. Just some smart-arse journalist on Twitter criticising us as usual." He flashed a toothy smile at Rachel, who flicked her head down at the open folder. "Anyway, a couple more months and I won't have to deal with imbeciles anymore. Peace and bloody quiet down at the caravan in Wales. That's what I'm looking forward to."

"I don't blame you, sir."

Jenkins smiled and tapped the edge of her desk. "Don't you be staying too late either. I need fresh soldiers," He turned and left Rachel to it.

"Night, sir," Rachel called after him. She pinched the bridge of her nose and, realising Jenkins was right, closed the folder and decided to go home. After clicking off her light and pulling her office door shut, she noticed, with it now being darker in the incident room, that a blue screen light was the only patch of illumination the room. Curious, she walked over.

"Hi, Tina. It's rare anyone stays later than I do. Busy?"

Tina Saunders looked up from her screen. "No, not really. I'm just catching up with some case files and typing them up. I've got a fundraiser tonight at my church and it's closer to here than it is home, so I thought I'd use my time productively. I've got my supplies." Tina tipped her head towards a little red travel mug and a bread roll wrapped in cellophane.

"That's a nice cushion," Rachel said, noticing it tucked between the back of the chair and Tina's ample behind.

"Oh, I had it made from my late husband's favourite shirt. I can still smell him on it, even though he's been gone over two years now." Tina's wide grin faded. "I like to think he's still with me when I have this cushion near me."

"And are those your grandchildren?" Rachel nodded towards a cluster of photographs pinned to the dividing wall between Tina's cubicle and the one next to it.

"Yes, they're my little monkeys. I can't wait to go down to two days a week soon. I can spend more time with them then. Oh, I love my job and all that, but there's more to life, don't you think? And the kids at that great age where they like to do everything, you know? They're my world. Especially since Donald passed. Do you have children?" Rachel shook her head. "Oh, well, you're still young. There's time for you yet."

"Do you need a lift to the church or anything, Tina? I can hang on half an hour or so," Rachel said.

"Oh, no, thank you. I like the walk. Especially at this lovely time of year. It's only ten minutes away. You get yourself home. Like you say, you're always staying here late. But it's more than a lot do around here, if you don't mind my saying. You're showing the other detectives up with your dedication."

Chapter 11

THE DRIVE UP to Liverpool had been a long one. Finally, after six long hours, stopping at services for breaks every few hours, and hitting heavy rush hour traffic on the M6, even though she'd set off at 4 a.m., Katie pulled up outside the Travelodge in Aigburth she'd booked for the night. Remembering she couldn't check in until 12 p.m., she pulled back onto the leafy, tree-lined dual carriageway and followed the road into Liverpool City centre.

Everything she passed seemed unfamiliar to her. There were shiny new retail parks, which understandably were different, but even when she got nearer to the city centre, the high rises and listed buildings, ones that had been there for centuries, let alone the decades Katie had been away for, looked as alien to her as if she had landed on another planet, let alone her home town. The enormous reddish-brown bricked Anglican cathedral on a hill in the distance was so gigantic it seemed to scrape the clear, blue sky with the crown of long, stone thorns on its square-topped central tower. But it wasn't just the feeling of strangeness that hit Katie, it was also the lack of emotion she felt for her home city. She pulled over outside the cathedral, set her sat nav for Jenny's house and carried on her way.

Outside Jenny's semi-detached house in the leafy suburb of Woolton, Katie saw no cars on the drive. The driveway gate was pulled shut and there seemed to be no signs of life. She decided to pull away and drive around a bit, to see if anything she passed triggered even the vaguest memory. Driving back down Beaconsfield Road, she passed a large, gated school on the right, with a high sandstone perimeter wall, but it looked as nondescript as any. On the left, further down the road, even the bright red wrought iron gate of Strawberry Field, and the various colours in the graffiti on the sandstone gate posts, stirred not even a flicker of a memory to her. Nor did Calderstones Park—which she came to next after crossing Menlove Avenue—despite the enormous boating lake within its expansive grounds. Finally, she turned back on herself, making the decision to sit outside Jenny's house and wait for her to return home.

Stopping at a corner shop in Allerton on the way, to pick up a newspaper to read while she waited, Katie had a first heart-pounding memory flood back to her. *I've been here*, she thought. Stepping out of her car, she walked into the corner shop and browsed while she waited for the shopkeeper to finish with his customer. When he did so, Katie walked up to him, her face creased into a frown of recognition when she saw up close the dark red port wine stain birthmark on his cheek she'd remembered seeing when she was little.

"Hi. Um… Can I ask you something?" She waited for the shopkeeper to imply his permission. "Are you Liam Porter's dad?"

The shopkeeper looked her in the eye and waited a moment before nodding. "I am. Who are you?"

Katie beamed, relieved she'd remembered something accurately. "I'm Katie. Katie Spencer. Me and your Liam were mates in class. We were only six or seven. I remember you picking him up after school while I waited for my dad. And I used to come in here for—."

Katie had been wittering on so long that she hadn't

noticed the darkness that had crossed Mr. Porter's unshaven chubby face. His features folded into a fierce glare.

"I know who you are. I remember. Get the *fuck* out of my shop. Get out of my shop, now!" he yelled, banging his palms down hard on the counter, making the bottles in the fridge next to him rattle together.

Katie's whole body froze in shock. After he screamed in her face again, she finally snapped into action, running out of the door and over to the safety of her car. Once inside, she pressed the central locking button and sat in stunned silence for the next ten minutes.

———

"Morning, boss," Chloe Sharp called out from behind Rachel as she followed her into the office. Rachel looked round and saw her beaming smile. "You cycled in again today?" Chloe nodded down to the helmet Rachel was carrying in her hand.

"Yeah. Seemed such a nice morning for it," Rachel replied.

"I go out most weekends on my bike. It's a really nice ride around Sefton Park. We could meet there at the Palm House one Saturday, if you're interested?" Chloe's bright blue eyes looked hopeful of a yes. Rachel flashed a polite smile and nodded her 'maybe'. She looked past Chloe and saw Mags approaching, laden with paperwork, with two coffee cups rested precariously on top. Mags stopped and looked down at the cups.

"Oh, Christ, Steve. I think I've put milk in your coffee again. And it was two sugars, wasn't it, Mark?"

The two grey-suited DCs that lifted their heads up from their computers when their names were called flashed weary smiles at Mags. One, with black short hair and a stubble beard, reached up to take his coffee.

"Thanks, Mags. I'm sure it'll be fine with the sugar in."
He whispered to Steve next to him, "Swap you?"

Mags held out Steve's incorrect order, and as she turned to
walk away both men switched cups, took a swig and gave
Mags a thumbs up when she turned back around to sit down
at her desk.

"She always gets it wrong," Chloe said out of the corner
of her mouth to Rachel. "I don't know how; she makes them
a brew every morning. They reckon she's going senile."

Jenkins swept past Rachel on his way over to his office in
the corner. "Morning, Rachel," he said as he walked past. By
the time Rachel looked back at the scene in front of her,
Chloe was looking down at her phone.

"What do you think?" Chloe said showing Rachel her
phone and watching her reaction closely. "Swipe right or left?"

"Um…he looks a bit weedy. You'd kick his arse with all that
kickboxing you do," Rachel replied, remembering back to their
conversations over their Chinese when they stayed late last week.
"No, Sharp. You need someone with a bit more about them than
Mr. Bean there," she said, pointing at the guy on the screen.

Chloe blushed. "I guess so. I'm like you in that way. Like
someone to look after me, but keep me on my toes as well. Is
your husband like that?" The words tumbled out of Chloe's
mouth before she registered where she was and who she was
talking to. "Oh, sorry. I shouldn't have said that. That was way
too personal. And we're at work. Shit." Chloe floundered,
until Rachel laid a hand on her shoulder.

"Don't worry. Things with me and Adam are…strange at
the moment. But what will be, will be. If it's worth having, it
can't be rushed."

Chloe nodded.

"But let's keep the private conversations for after work,
shall we?" Rachel added. Chloe nodded again, her cheeks still
a little pink.

"Morning, ladies," Tina Saunders said as she walked up

behind Rachel and Chloe. "Now, who's for a nice bit of shortbread?"

"Lovely," Chloe said, dipping her fingers into the open tin Tina was offering out. She took a bite and licked the crumbs off her lips, catching the others in her hand.

"Thanks, Tina. Glad I cycled in now. It makes this guilt-free," Rachel said, also taking a piece of crumbly shortbread. "You're terrible for my figure with all these treats you bring in."

"Oh, don't be silly," Tina said. "I'd kill for your figure at my age. Don't you think so, Chloe?"

Chloe nodded.

Tina put the lid back on her tin. "But shhhh, don't tell Mags about me playing mum. She'll think I'm stepping on her toes." She tapped her nose and returned to her desk.

MR. PORTER'S tirade had caused Katie to sit in stunned silence in her car. Thoughts tumbled around in her head. *He must have me confused with somebody else*, she thought. *What on Earth could he think I've done to deserve that reaction?* It wasn't his words as much as the look of wide-eyed horror on his face that freaked her out the most. She drove back down the only other road to Jenny's that she could remember. Hancock Street. Moments later, she had pulled up outside her child-hood home. As she looked at the Victorian semi-detached, with its black and white painted apex roof, solid red brick exterior and white-painted mullion windows with stained glass in the top portion, a shiver ran down her spine. She took off her seatbelt, got out of the car and walked up the long, angled driveway and past the shrubs that edged it.

"Can I help you, love?" a voice called out from the front drive of next door.

Katie looked over the hedge to see a grizzled, wild-haired old lady, looking back at her through inquisitive blue eyes. She was wearing a worn, brown cardigan, dark green wool skirt and brown fluffy slippers. An off-white and blue striped apron was wrapped around her waist, covered with what looked like flour. She stood poised for an answer, her forehead inclined.

"Umm…hi. I used to live here. Years ago," Katie replied, then focused her eyes more carefully on the nosy old lady. "It's…Mrs. Parker, isn't it?" Katie faintly remembered.

"Who's asking?" the old woman replied, folding her arms over her apron. Her loose permed white hair bobbed as she spoke.

"My name's Katie. Katie Spencer. Do you remember me? I lived here about twenty years ago." Katie pointed behind her.

Mrs. Parker recoiled. Across her face fell a shadow of pure shock. After a few seconds she spoke, her hostile voice more shaky now. "What? What the bleeding hell are you doing back here?" she said, her voice tapering out to a whisper.

Katie spread her arms. "I'm not sure, really. I came back up here to visit my sister. You remember Jenny? She's a couple of years older than me. And I thought I'd come and see my old house."

The haggard old lady continued to glare at Katie. "Does anyone else know you're here?"

"Not really. I left my sister a voicemail earlier to ask her if I could come round, or she could come to my hotel. I left it up to her to decide. Oh, I spoke to the father of some lad I used to know in the shop up the road." Katie stopped. "But he looked at me like you're looking at me now. Why did you ask who knew I was here? What's going on here?"

"Look, I think you should get back in your car and go back to wherever it is you came from. Things around here have only just got back to normal." Mrs. Parker wrung her hands and fiddled with the cord of her apron as she spoke. She looked around at the houses along the street to see if anyone else had come out.

"Normal?" Katie said, wrinkling her brow. "What the hell

is that supposed to mean?" Her patience was running out, not able to get a straight answer from the old lady.

"You don't remember?" Mrs. Parker replied. Katie looked at her and shook her head.

"No." Katie's eyes moistened and the old lady's harsh exterior softened slightly.

"Oh, bleeding hell. You'd better come in then. Quickly though, before anyone sees you loitering about the place. Last thing I want is you causing mither."

———

Rachel had been standing at the top of the steep concrete steps outside the police station for half an hour on the phone to her mum. Breathing the fresh air in, she leaned against the black metal railing listening while her mum told her all about her shopping trip to Newquay, before finally getting a word in edgewise.

"Work's fine, Mum. Really. Yes, I'm taking it easy. Well, as easy as you know I can. Everyone's great. Apart from one of my DCs, who seems to be on the 'I don't give a crap' train. But you can't have it all perfect. OK, Mum, you just enjoy your afternoon tea. Say hi to Glynis for me. Love you. Bye."

"There you are," Chloe said, appearing from the door behind her. Rachel pocketed her phone and turned around.

"Everything OK in there?" Rachel asked.

Chloe smiled and breathed in the air. On the ground at the bottom of the steps, a pair of seagulls squared up to each other, squawking and screeching as they fought over a small pile of squashed chips. "Yeah. Just thought I'd get some fresh air too. Felt a bit cabin fever-y in there this morning. My mum always used to say stagnant air breeds stagnant thoughts. Not what we need when we've got cases to solve. And Bradley's aftershave was giving me a headache." She laughed, as did Rachel.

"I know. He has laid the old Paco Rabanne on a bit thick,

hasn't he? I think he's got a bit of a crush on you. Mags thinks so too. She was banging on about it before."

Chloe blushed. "You think? Hmm…I'm not really interested in him."

Rachel rocked on her heels and combed her hair back with her fingers. "Oh, I don't know. He seems nice enough. It gets you off those dating sites? You should give him a chance."

"No," Chloe replied. Rachel snapped her head back at the bluntness of Chloe's response. "Sorry. Didn't mean to sound harsh. I just…I know when I'm not interested in someone."

"Fair enough."

"Anyway, I've decided to stay after work for the next few nights to get on with sorting out the timelines for the Davies case."

"How have you got on so far? Anything new caught your eye? Nobody else on the team had any thoughts at all?" Rachel quipped.

"Well, there are four possibilities as to what happened to Callum. I narrowed it down from all the other red herrings, so that's what I'll be doing this afternoon and tonight."

"Nice one, good effort."

They walked back into the police station and headed back up to the incident room. When they got there, Mags was chatting animatedly to Bradley, who laughed loudly at her punchline.

"Right, everyone, let's go into my office and have a catch up on what we've discovered over the course of this morning." She looked at Chloe. "I'll get you to start if that's OK, Sharp?"

"Of course," Chloe replied, the sense of pride swelling in her chest.

Once inside Rachel's office, and seated around her briefing table, Chloe opened her notebook and began to list off the four possibilities she'd deduced from the evidence she'd gone through with a fine-toothed comb. Once she'd finished, she looked at Rachel who gave her a nod of approval. But Mags gave her a slow hand clap.

"Well, get *you*, Chloe Sharp, showing us all how it's done," Mags said with a smile. "I definitely won't be missed around here, will I?"

Chloe laughed, then looked at Mags, sensing the edge in her voice and a cold look in her eyes she hadn't ever seen before.

After Bradley had gone through his telephone conversations and door-to-door enquiries, Rachel called the meeting to a close. Mags and Bradley stood up and collected their notes and headed back to their desks. Chloe remained seated, her expression blank as she stared at the wall.

"Everything OK, Sharp?" Rachel asked.

"Yeah. It's just what Mags said before. I don't know whether to take it as a compliment or not."

"Who knows with Mags? She's a funny one, that's for sure. I sometimes don't quite know where I stand. But if you feel she's being funny with you, you come and tell me. OK?" Rachel perched on the corner of her desk and folded her arms.

Chloe looked up from the briefing table and smiled. "Thank you. I appreciate that. I know I'm only young, and I've got a hell of a lot to learn about this job. But I'm not still some trainee detective just waiting to be signed off as substantive. I studied hard and passed that exam after two years' hard graft. I don't want to be taken the piss out of. You know? It's bad enough when your own father thinks you're too blonde and stupid to be a copper, without me taking it from Mags too."

"You're overthinking." Rachel said. "And sod what your dad thinks. And Mags, for that matter. I happen to think you're doing a sterling job. And I've passed that on to Jenkins, and Clifford as well. So you just put all negative thoughts out of your head, OK?"

Chloe replied with a half-smile of appreciation at the pep

talk. "You're right. I mean, I like Mags, but I won't let her make me feel stupid. Not when I'm working so bloody hard." Chloe's meek demeanour had switched back now into the feisty, take-no-shit woman Rachel had come to really like.

"Right then. Now get back out there, hold your head up and crack on."

"I will." Chloe stood up and walked over to the door. She turned back and flashed Rachel a warm smile.

Outside the office, Tina was standing talking to Bradley.

"How's the church fundraising going, Tina?" Rachel asked as she stood in the doorway.

"Oh, it's going great. We raised £250 last week just on the cake sale alone," Tina gushed.

"Well, that doesn't surprise me, Tina. Your cakes are amazing." Rachel replied, smiling.

"I'll second that," Bradley chipped in as he munched on one of the cookies that Tina had brought in yesterday and wiped the crumbs off his tie.

"Did you want me?" Rachel asked Tina, realising that she had been waiting outside her office. She nodded at Bradley to get back to his desk.

"Oh, yes. I was going to ask if you wanted me to drop you some tea round tonight? I know you're still settling into your new house, and I always make too much scouse. It's no trouble."

Rachel smiled and shook her head. "Thank you, Tina. That's very kind. But I'll be fine. You do enough by keeping me going with your cakes."

"OK then, but you just say if you ever want a care package bringing in. Promise?"

Rachel looked at Tina, taking in her kind eyes and motherly aura. "I will. Now, let's crack on, shall we?"

———

Katie sat in Mrs. Parker's living room. She had been ushered to sit down in a worn brown armchair while the old woman came back with some tea. The room hadn't been decorated since the mid-nineties. It had peeling beige wallpaper and dark oak wood everywhere. There was a dark green three-seater sofa, its armrests almost threadbare, along the longest wall in the room and through the archway at the far end was a small alcove room with a mahogany dining table covered in ornaments. At the back was a Welsh dresser stacked with plates of all different colours and patterns. The living room carpet was a greeny-brown colour with swirl patterns, worn away at the edges of the brass carpet grips in the doorway.

"Here we are," Mrs. Parker said as she returned to the living room with a small brown tray laden with two chipped mugs of dark brown tea. "Sorry it's dark. Milk's on the turn." She sat down and offered Katie a mug.

"When did he die, Mrs. Parker?"

"Oh, call me Pam. I can't be arsed with all that formality." She sipped her tea. "Four years ago now. I just assumed Jenny would have told you. I would have, but I didn't have your address or phone number for where you'd be now. It was all very hush hush when you left all those years ago. One or two?"

Katie refocused her eyes on Pam who was holding out a sugar bowl and a teaspoon. "I don't normally, but better make it two," she said, letting Pam drop the heaped teaspoons of sugar in her mug. "I don't understand. Why didn't anyone tell me my father had died? Did they not think I deserved to know? I'm so confused."

"I'm sorry, love. That must have been hard to just be told like that."

"I don't understand any of this. All I remember is my mum died when I was five and my dad couldn't cope with me and Jenny, so sent me to live with my Auntie Joan in Brighton when I was seven. As I got older I kind of understood why he did it, and I didn't blame him. But Jenny has been really weird with me for as long as I can remember, and then, as soon as I come back here and speak to a shopkeeper whose son I used to play with when I was little, he yells at me and kicks me out of his shop. What the hell is going on here, Pam?"

Pam took a deep breath and sipped her tea. "I'm sure Colin Porter didn't mean anything by it. It's just… Well, for a while after you left, businesses suffered with all the press poking around the area. This neighbourhood was all over the news back then. Gave it a right bad name, all that attention."

Katie shook her head. "Bad name? Pam, you're not getting to the point." She leaned forward in her armchair. "Why?"

"Bleeding hell, queen. You serious that nobody's ever told you?"

"Told me what?"

—————————

Chapter 12

—————————

CHLOE SHARP BURST into Rachel's office clutching a piece of paper, her eyes as bright as the crisp white shirt she was wearing. Her blonde hair fell across her jubilant face as the breeze from Rachel's open window caught it.

"I'll let you off the lack of a good honest knock, Sharp, if you tell me what's put that smile on your face," Rachel said after looking up from her computer screen.

"I found him. Well, I found two candidates from all the ones on the database who fitted the age and description," Chloe said, barely drawing breath.

"Who?" Rachel replied, trying to keep up.

"Callum Davies. I've spoken to one of them already, who pretty much told me to piss off as he didn't have a clue what I was talking about, and the other one didn't answer his phone. But, judging by the info I've got on the second one, I reckon he's our missing person. We need to double check though."

Rachel grinned. "Excellent work, Sharp. Well done."

"Thanks. But, if I'm being honest, this wasn't a particularly difficult case to crack. Just needed some good old-fashioned police work. Following up statements, reading between the lines, etc...."

"Well, considering the calibre of who work here, hardly

surprising," Rachel muttered. She looked back up at Chloe who stood smiling down at her like a proud puppy. "Right, well, shall we go and see him then to tie up the case?"

"See who?" Supt. Jenkins piped up from the doorway. Chloe turned round.

"Callum Davies," Rachel replied, looking round Chloe at her boss. "A young lad who's been missing this past year. Sharp, here, has been like a dog with a bone trying to follow up leads to locate him. She's got to the bottom of it and found him, so we think. We need to pay a visit to confirm, but it's looking good. Right, Sharp?"

"Hopefully," Chloe replied.

Jenkins reached over to slap Chloe on the shoulder. "Right, well, congratulations, DC Sharp. I knew you'd be an excellent addition to the team. Great to see you're putting your training into action." He looked back at Rachel with a mock frown. "I hope you're utilising DC Chapman on this too? I'm not paying detective rates for her to sit on her behind all day playing Candy Crush." He jutted his head to indicate over his shoulder, where Rachel could see Mags scrolling through her phone.

"Of course, sir. I'll brief the team on our progress in a few minutes."

Jenkins nodded. "Good, good. Otherwise she'll only start complaining to me about feeling like we're putting her out to grass already." He thought for a moment. "Actually, I think she should go and follow up on this Callum Davies? No need for a DI to go, and Sharp, you've already done enough for the team."

Rachel balked. Chloe looked at her with hopeful eyes. "Sir? If you're sending a DC then I think Sharp should get the opportunity to wrap this up, seeing as though she was the one who did all the work," Rachel said, adding the last sentence as Jenkins turned around and waved Mags over.

"Nonsense. Let's share out the workload, eh?" Jenkins replied.

Chloe spread her hands but Rachel shushed her.

"Chapman, over here," Jenkins yelled over to Mags, who trotted over. "Mags, DC Sharp has done some sterling work tracking down Callum Davies and because of the size of the case load, to help DI Morrison out, could you take down all the details from Sharp here and go and confirm it is the correct Callum Davies?"

Mags stepped back in surprise. "We've found him? I didn't even know…"

"I was about to brief you," Rachel replied. "I've only just this minute found out myself."

"There we are then," Jenkins said with a satisfied grin. "An excellent team result. Sharp, Morrison, onto the next case. DC Chapman, get yourself over to Davies' place and box this one off, will you?"

"Yes, sir," Mags replied, following him as he strode away from Rachel's office doorway.

"Sorry, Sharp," Rachel murmured. "That one should have been yours."

"That's OK," Chloe replied in a quiet voice, her face downcast. "On to the next one, eh?" She walked slowly back over to her desk.

KATIE HAD BEEN STARING at a damp patch on Pam's wood chipped wallpaper for the last few minutes since the old woman's bombshell announcement. She squeezed out her voice. "What?"

Pam reached forward and clasped her hand over Katie's. "I know it's come as a bit of a shock to you. I'm sorry."

"I have a little sister? Why wasn't I told about her? Where is she now? Does Jenny know about her?" The questions tumbled out of Katie's mouth as quickly as they'd flown through her brain.

Pam put her coffee cup down and shifted uncomfortably

in her seat. "Oh Jesus. I don't know… I don't even know how to say this…"

Katie glared at Pam. "Just say it, for God's sake."

"OK." Pam smoothed down the creases in her lap and set her face as she thought of her next sentence. "There were three of yous. Jenny, you and your little sister. Her name was Mollie."

Katie's whole body shuddered. "Mollie? That's the name of the little girl Jenny had a picture of in her phone case. She *knew* about her?"

"Well, of course she did," Pam replied.

Katie sat back in her chair, trying to process what she'd heard. "What a cow. I've been calling her and sending her messages. I've been Facebooking her friends because she's not returning my calls. For God's sake, this shows how much of a complete idiot I am. I thought this Mollie was a child Jenny had lost or something, and that's why she didn't want to speak to me about her. We've never been that close as sisters, so I understood her feelings about that, but I never thought… I was trying to be really sympathetic, and all this time…"

Katie could feel her blood boiling as she went over and over in her head Jenny's coldness towards her back in Brighton. She stood up and began pacing the room.

"I've got a little sister I never even knew about, kept from me for all this time by a sister that seems to hate me for some reason? Do you know how lonely I've felt all my life, being stuck down in Brighton all by myself? Removed from my family because my dad couldn't cope with the two of us? And there were *three* of us? That means my dad kept Jenny and Mollie, and sent *me* away. Why? Why me? What did I do that was so wrong to be sent hundreds of miles away? And why don't I remember Mollie? Why doesn't Mollie contact *me*?"

Pam raised her palms. "Katie, please. Please try to calm down. I'll tell you everything, but you have to calm down a bit. The neighbours."

"Fuck the neighbours. I want to know why my dad

couldn't cope with three of us but could cope with two. And why my so-called sister never even told me my dad had fucking died. What the *hell* is going on here?" Katie punctuated the last part of her sentence with finger jabs down on the mahogany coffee table. Seeing Pam's shocked face, she sat down slowly and tried to compose herself. "I'm sorry, Pam. It's just…I feel all of a sudden I don't know my own family anymore. Everything I thought I knew is a total lie."

"I can understand how you feel. It must be a terrible shock."

"That's an understatement, Pam." Katie locked eyes with the old lady. "Where is Mollie now?"

Pam pressed her wrinkly hand to her mouth and closed her eyes. "Oh, bleeding hell."

"Pam?"

"I'm sorry. But Mollie's dead."

Her words hit Katie like a clutch of sharp stones.

"What? When? How?"

"When she was five. You had just turned seven and Jenny was ten. You and Mollie were playing together in the back garden, Jenny was next door and one day Mollie fell. She broke her neck on the wooden decking from height, bashed her head and died."

"Oh my God. But why don't I remember that?" Katie's eyes filled up with tears. "What does that have to do with people being angry at *me*?"

Pam looked away and dabbed her eyes with a crumpled-up tissue. She looked back at Katie, her face set hard. "Because…you pushed her."

Chapter 13

AFTER NEGOTIATING her sky-blue Audi A1 around the grim, one-way streets of Kensington, Mags parked up just after a wide speed hump, outside a rundown three-storey red-bricked terraced house, in a street where several of the adjacent properties were boarded up. It was only four miles away from Callum Davies' family home, but the surrounding area was worlds apart from the pleasant, leafy suburb of Aigburth where he'd grown up. Mags checked the address in her notebook and, confident she'd got the right house, locked her car and walked over to the dark green front door. She laid three heavy knocks on the paint-chipped wood, which opened.

"Yeah?" a hooded black youth muttered through the tiny crack in the door. A waft of sickly sweet air blew towards Mags from behind him.

Mags smiled. "Hi. Is Callum in?"

"Who's askin'?"

Mags held up her warrant card, her fixed smile remaining on her perfectly made up face. "Get Callum for me, lad, and I'll ignore the green I can smell on you."

The youth rolled his eyes and leaned back to call over his shoulder. "Cal. Door. It's the bizzies."

Mags looked up and down the street waiting, but Callum

91

didn't appear. Impatient, she hammered on the door again. "Callum, I know you're in there. You want your mate to get done for possession?"

Callum appeared at the door, frowning. He was unshaven, with dark circles around his dull blue eyes. He had a black sweatshirt on, with the hood pulled up around his head. His grey sweatpants were grubby, his trainers worn at the toes. "What?" he growled.

"Callum Davies?"

"Who are you?"

"DC Chapman, Merseyside Police," Mags said, taking out her warrant card again and showing it to him before putting it back in her trench coat pocket. "You were reported missing. Quite a while ago, actually. I've been sent to check you're alive and kicking."

"So now you've seen, you can fuck off again." Callum went to slam the door, but Mags reached up to stop it closing.

"No need to be like that, Callum," she said in her most motherly tone. "Look, I'm just here to make sure you're OK and to see if you need anything. There are a fair few people worrying about you, you know, disappearing in the middle of the night like that? Leaving your trainer by the dockside? And your baby's really missing his daddy. I've met him. He's beautiful. Got your eyes, he has."

Callum sniffed and wiped his nose on the back of his grubby fist.

"We care about your welfare, Callum," Mags continued. "There are people out there who haven't given up on you. Courtney, for one. And little Tommy."

"How did you find me?" Callum asked, his eyes nervously scanning the distance behind her.

"We're good at our job," Mags replied, to which Callum snorted. His stare hardened.

"Good at your job? That's a fuckin' joke," he added in a mocking tone. "Piss off, pig." He went to close the door again, but Mags held up a hand in annoyance.

"Callum, love. I'm not here for a row. You're old enough to make your own decisions on your life. Our only concern was that you were safe and well, and not at the bottom of Canning Dock. Now I can see that, I'm obligated to ask you if you need any support or want us to put you in contact with anyone who can provide you with housing or counselling for the reason you left your family. Or, I could fuck off and say you declined support and you said you were fine. If that's what you really want."

Callum locked eyes with Mags, trying to weigh up whether her soft tone reassured or terrified him. "Yeah, that second one. I just wanna be left alone, OK? And I don't want you lot telling Courtney or my dad where I am. I mean it." He pulled the sleeves of his sweatshirt over his hands and wrapped his arms around his skinny body.

"OK then, Callum. You take care of yourself."

Mags let go of the door, letting Callum slam it shut. She walked back over to her car and climbed inside. Opening up her notebook, she drew a bold cross over Callum's name and snapped the notebook shut with a deep sigh.

———

PAM PLACED a fresh tray of tea and chocolate biscuits down on the coffee table. It had been twenty minutes since her revelation to Katie, and the air had been thick ever since.

"I don't even know how I could have killed Mollie. I don't even remember her, let alone killing her," Katie said in disbelief. She nursed the cup that Pam had handed her before taking a slow sip.

"It was years ago, Katie. Many years ago. I mean, I don't know all the info myself really. The police'll know that, but… between speaking to your dad, and his best mate, Bill Thompson, who was there and saw it happen, well, the general feeling was that you and Mollie just never got on."

"Who told you that?"

"Your dad. Bill was over the house all the time and told the police and some journalists that you hated Mollie all along, and that's why you did what you did."

"They think I did it on purpose? Like, premeditated? Christ. No wonder everyone from here thinks I'm a monster. Pam, what did I do? How exactly did Mollie die?"

"You remember the cabin shed at the far end of your back garden?"

Katie shook her head. "Not clearly, anyway. I recognised the front of the house, vaguely. Enough to know it as soon as I drove up to it again. But I don't remember the garden."

Pam shook her head. "I'm not surprised, love. You've probably blocked it out. The trauma must have affected you too. Well, at the bottom of your garden is a cabin shed built on stilts. Your dad used to call it the 'man cave'. Mollie was playing on the top step of the decking area which was quite a few feet off the ground. Apparently, you…pushed her off. She broke her neck on the steps on the way down and died instantly. Your dad saw you out the window standing next to her just before she fell. Said you pushed her. Bill witnessed it from inside the cabin looking out the window, saying he'd heard you shouting at Mollie seconds before she fell."

"This is unreal. I don't remember any of this. Where was Jenny when I supposedly did this?"

"She was next door and came running over with the neighbours when they all heard the commotion. I was walking back from the shops at the time. I followed the noise and saw everybody, the ambulance, the police. It was a horrible sight."

"But why didn't anyone tell me about it? I know I was young at the time, but this was twenty years ago."

"Because of your age, and the fact that it was deemed as an 'accidental death', nobody was allowed to speak to you about it, as the counsellors and family liaison officers said it would cause you trauma. But the press got wind of what had happened, no doubt paying people to talk, and they camped out in the town while they gathered local knowledge and initially put their own spin on the facts. Anything to sell rags. They interviewed neighbours but were forbidden to interview your family or print anything with your name in to protect you. But it was an open secret. It didn't stop people talking about it just because they couldn't read about it."

"I Googled my name when you were in the kitchen and couldn't find anything."

"The press had one of them, what they called? 'Embargo' thingies. They weren't allowed, on court orders, to report anything directly because of your age and the nature of the incident. So, the press was annoyed they couldn't print their headlines. It was a different time back then. Social media didn't exist either, so you wouldn't have seen anything about it on there. The local businesses were annoyed at the unwanted attention from rubberneckers visiting the town. No one could break the embargo, but enough was inferred by local tittle-tattle to make it impossible for you to stay here. They were worried for your safety."

"That's why Jenny doesn't want to have a relationship with me. That's why she doesn't want me to have a relationship with my niece. Oh my God, does she think I'd do the same to Charlotte? What kind of a monster does she think I am?" Katie's tears were streaming down her face now.

"Oh, Katie, I'm so sorry," Pam said as she passed her the box of tissues she had by her sofa.

"Why are *you* being so nice to me?" Katie asked, blowing her nose.

"I know what it's like to have people treat you not very nicely." Her eyes met with Katie's and she smiled. "Oh, I know what everyone around here calls me. 'Nosey Parker Pam'. Just because I like to keep a look out at who's on my street, doesn't make me a bad person. But they still stare. They still accuse and call me names in the street. So I kind of understand."

"Our crimes are worlds apart, though, Pam. Aren't they?"

"You were only a kid. It was an accident."

They sat in silence. Pam looked up at the clock on the mantelpiece. Katie had been there well over an hour now. Katie saw her look at the clock and recovered herself. "I should leave you in peace now. I've taken up enough of your day. But thank you, Pam. For being the only one around here to be honest with me."

They both stood up and walked over to the front door.

"Are you sure you're OK?" Pam asked.

"Yeah. I just don't know what I'm going to tell my boyfriend. I work in a nursery. What the hell am I going to tell *them*?"

Pam looked at her and clasped her hand. "Maybe you should just keep it to yourself."

———

RACHEL LOOKED up from her computer after a knock at her door snapped her out of her concentrated stare.

"I spoke to Callum Davies," Mags said. "It was the right one. He's fine. He just wants to be left alone to get on with his life. He said he's fine with us closing the missing person's file on him."

Rachel frowned. "That's it? He goes missing for over a year, without letting his family, not to mention his then-pregnant girlfriend, know? Did he say why he didn't get in contact with anybody?"

Mags shook her head. "I didn't ask. He didn't seem like he wanted to talk about it."

Rachel stared at her.

"Is there a problem?" Mags asked, placing a hand on her hip.

"A young bloke with a pregnant girlfriend, just upping and leaving is hardly new, but leaving a shoe on the dockside, as if faking his own death? Just seems a bit extreme. He really wanted his family to believe he was dead. Not just missing."

Mags shrugged. "Maybe he thought his kid was better off

without him? To be honest, he didn't look like he had a lot going for him when I met him, poor thing. Anyway, it's Social's job now to chase him for child support, not us. Don't overthink it and make life harder on yourself by looking for something that isn't there. I've been in this game long enough to know that you can't save them all, no matter how much you might want to. It's sad, yes. But Callum Davies is a thirty-two-year-old adult. He can decide what he wants. If he doesn't want Courtney or his dad to find out where he is then that's his right. And we have to respect that decision. I'll let the gang know we're moving on to the next case."

Chapter 14

Still in shock from what Pam had told her, Katie wasn't in any fit state to drive. A maelstrom of thoughts still swirled around in her head before one came to the forefront. If Pam still lived in the street, maybe Bill did too?

She walked to the end of Pam's driveway and looked up the length of the street, one side then the other, looking for a house that triggered any kind of memory. One house in particular, five doors up on the opposite side of the road, stuck out to her. There was a silver Vauxhall Astra in the driveway, a hopeful sign that someone was home, Katie thought. She walked across the road and up to the cobbled driveway, passing a little stone wishing well water feature a few yards from the black-painted heavy oak front door. She rang the doorbell and took in a deep breath as she waited. There was no answer, so she rang again. She heard footsteps. There was a rattle of a security chain still connected as the door opened a crack.

"I'm not interested," came a gruff voice from a short, middle-aged man with a thin, scowling face.

"Are you Bill Thompson?" Katie asked, peering through the crack in hope that she would recognise him.

"Who wants to know?"

"I'm Katie, Katie Spencer. You knew my dad…Peter." Katie was too weary for any preamble.

The figure behind the door seemed to shrink. The gruff voice had fallen silent.

"Hello? Mr. Thompson? Can we talk, please? I need to ask you some questions, if that would be alright?" Katie persisted.

"You need to go. Now. I don't want you on my property," Bill replied. His voice was now pinched into a fearful whinge.

"I won't stay long. I just need to know what happened to Mollie. Look, I'm not going anywhere until I speak to you, and I *can* cause a scene if you'd prefer?"

Katie's threat had the desired effect. The chain slid off and the door opened. Bill was wearing a tatty wool cardigan, dirty light blue jeans and brown loafers. Clearly in need of a bath and a shave, his stench hit Katie full in the face as a light breeze blew down his hallway from the open back kitchen door. His dark brown malicious eyes glared at her and his lip curled into a snarl, revealing long, sharp, yellow teeth.

"Listen here, I remember you. Don't you dare come here threatening me, or I'll have the bizzies on you. You're not welcome here, so fuck off." He prodded a cigarette-stained finger in Katie's face.

"Please. Just give me a few minutes to explain. I don't remember anything about what happened when I was a kid. I've only just been told about it."

"The rest of us around here remember. I ain't going through all that shit again. Poor little kid. Just lying there, she was. Head all split open, neck bent." His dark eyes became glassy as he stared into space while he remembered. He refocused on Katie. "You did that. You."

"Where was my dad when it happened?"

"In the cabin shed watching the footie. We both were. I saw what happened through the window. Heard a terrifying scream that I won't ever forget and there she was on the ground. You stood there on the decking looking down at her over the broken railing. The look of evil on your face."

Katie shook her head. "It just doesn't make any sense. I was only seven. Please, Mr. Thompson, can I come in for a few minutes?"

"No. I want to be left in peace now. You tore poor Pete's heart out that day. Mollie was his princess, his baby. He never got over it. Died a broken man, he did. My best mate. This street wasn't the same again. We were always known as 'the place where that little girl got killed'. But we weren't allowed to speak about Mollie, for fear of upsetting *you*. I'll never forgive you for what you did."

Katie burst into tears and pushed against the door. "I'm sorry, I'm so sorry. Please."

Bill gave her such a look of disgust and wrenched the door away from her as if he thought her touch was somehow poisoning the wood. Katie stumbled forward but Bill stepped back away from her. "It's way too late for sorry. Now get the fuck off my property, you murdering bitch." He slammed the door so hard the force of it nearly knocked Katie off her feet. She leaned back against the wall and held her head in her hands as the world spun around her. Eventually, after scraping herself up off the cold stone cobbles, she staggered back to her car. Once inside, she flicked the engine on and sped off, heading to the one place she knew she could finally get answers.

———

Sam had answered the hammering on the door.

"I want to see my sister!" Katie yelled. Jenny appeared in the hallway and blocked off the entrance.

"No, Katie. I'm not letting you in here. And lower your voice, please. I don't want Charlotte upset."

Sam moved his slight frame out of the way of the tornado that was his sister-in-law. He looked at Jenny with his arms spread. "What's going on, love?"

Jenny reached behind her to the hall table and grabbed

one of Charlotte's picture books. Taking the hint, Sam took his reading glasses out of his top shirt pocket and sauntered back into the living room.

"I know, Jenny. I know everything. I've been to see Pam. She told me what happened. I know about Mollie." Katie's words tumbled out as she waved her hands in Jenny's face.

"I need you to calm down, Katie. The whole avenue will be out on their doorsteps otherwise."

"Bollocks to that. I'm sick of everyone fobbing me off and shushing me. I want to know everything. Why didn't you tell me Dad had died? Did you not think I had a right to know? Or that I'd want to be at the funeral?"

Jenny lowered her head and exhaled. "I didn't want you to know he was dying. He didn't want to see you. He gave me 'power of attorney' so it was my responsibility to make sure his wishes were carried out. I'm assuming, as you've spoken to Nosey Parker Pam, that you know exactly why now?"

Sam came out of the living room, his brown eyes set hard. "Love, we can't have this on our doorstep. Either let her in, or tell her to go," he hissed at Jenny.

Katie softened her voice, the tears now rolling down her face. Her eyes searched around as if looking for answers. "Please, Jenny. Please talk to me. I'm so confused. I've done something unforgivable, I know. But I need your help. I can't remember what happened."

Jenny looked Katie dead in the eye, her lips hard. "That's the luxury *you* have. Because I can't ever forget. What I saw was horrific. Please go, and don't ever come back here again."

The door was slammed in her face. Overcome with emotion, Katie lurched forward and vomited into the shrubs bordering the path.

———

"Are you OK, madam?" the smartly dressed blonde receptionist asked as Katie, her expression vacant, walked up to the desk of the Travelodge hotel she'd booked a room at.

"I'm checking in," Katie replied, her tone flat.

"Name?"

"Katie Spencer."

The young receptionist tapped her bright red nails on the keyboard, locating Katie's booking, then handing her a room card. "First floor. Breakfast is between eight and ten. Checkout is ten-thirty. Do you need any help with your bags?" She looked over her desk down at Katie's feet but only saw one overnight bag. "Are you OK?"

"Yes. Thank you." Katie took the key card and set off up the stairs to her room. Once inside, she flopped onto the bed after dropping her bag to the floor. The tears soaked into the plump white pillow and drowned out the wails that followed. Then the screams came. Then the punches.

It all made sense now to Katie. Why she hadn't heard from her dad in so long. Why Jenny wanted nothing to do with her. Even her not being able to have anything to do with Charlotte became clear. *I'm a killer*, she thought. But, if it had been the other way around, would she have forgiven Jenny for killing Mollie? The inside of Katie's mind was a scene of complete and utter devastation. She got up from the bed and walked over to the bathroom. Feeling the cool splash of water on her face, she looked up at the mirror, despising what she saw. Her identity had changed. The red, blotchy face that stared back at her now was of a child killer. Unable to change what had happened, the road forward seemed a blur for Katie. What the hell was she supposed to do next? Her job in the nursery would have to end. Her relationship with Tom would likely be over. He'd never want to have a baby with her now. Not after this. She has killed somebody. She was completely responsible for somebody taking their last breath.

Her thoughts drifted to the day Mollie died. 'Died instantly', Bill had said. But was it painless? The noise of neck bones cracking ran through her head, causing her to vomit in the sink. *Why did I push her? And why didn't I run down where she fell, to help her?* "Why did I hate her so much to do this to her?" she shouted at the mirror, as drips of vomit ran down her chin. *Was my face the last thing she saw? I've killed somebody. I've actually caused somebody's death. I've ended somebody's life. I'm the reason somebody isn't walking around today. I'm the reason a whole town is talked about.* The room started to spin and she sank to the floor in breathless panic. Mollie had died thinking that her own sister hated her enough to watch her die.

Feeling a sudden sting, then throbbing sensation, Katie looked down at her forearms and realised she'd scratched long red lines down them, drawing blood in patches. Instead of running her arm under the tap, she picked at the deepest scratch until it wept even more sticky red blood. The force of her scratching made the glass on the side of the sink rock and then crash to the floor, smashing into long shards. Without thinking, she picked one up and dug it into her arm, gasping with agonising pain. But the pain released something else with it. A strange and all-consuming feeling of relief. Another cut followed, and another trickle of blood ran down her arm and pooled on the white tiled floor. Running out of clean, smooth skin on her forearm, Katie lifted up her t-shirt and slashed across her stomach, howling in pain. *Maybe this pain is what Mollie felt.* Before she'd truly comprehended what she'd done, every crisp white towel was stained with patches of blood.

It was dark by the time Katie opened her eyes again. She was lying on her side on the cold bathroom tiles, her face in what felt like a puddle of liquid. She lifted her head up and ran her fingers over her cheek and chin, then looked at her hand. It was scarlet. In the bedroom, her phone beeped, snapping her into the here and now. Staggering to her feet, she dragged her body over to the bed, trying where possible not to bleed all over the carpet. The towel she'd wrapped around her arm stemmed the bleeding enough for it not to drip.

"Hello?" she gasped, but the caller had already rung off.

Looking down at the call log, she saw it was from Tom. In no clear mind to speak to him, she staggered back to the bathroom and turned the shower on, to try and clean her wounds the best she could. Once she was clean and dry, she wrapped a towel around her mangled forearm and changed into a fresh t-shirt. She collapsed onto the bed, completely exhausted, and fell into a deep sleep.

———

It was almost nine o'clock when Rachel finally kicked her shoes off and relaxed back into the comfy cushions of her couch. The folders she'd been organising lay neatly on her coffee table and a glass of wine sat next to them. She reached for the wine glass and took a long, slow drink as she read a text message that had just come through. It was from Chloe. Rachel laughed as she played the video Chloe had sent her of a dog dressed up in police uniform looking like it was arresting a group of cats dressed as gangsters sitting in a black Ford Model 18 car. She messaged Chloe back and sipped at the wine again, laughing out loud when Chloe's witty reply came back. It felt nice to laugh, rather than sit at home feeling sad that she was alone, Rachel thought.

"Coming," she called out after the doorbell rang. Minutes later, she was back texting Chloe, but this time with her mouthful of sweet and sour chicken and Pickles purring in her lap.

You should come over one night, Chloe. You don't know what you're missing, Rachel texted, with a picture of her takeaway attached to the message.

Love to.

———

"Fucking hell, Katie. Where have you been? Why haven't you texted me back? I've been ringing you for hours!" Tom

104

yelled down the phone. Katie, in a complete haze, struggled to hold the phone to her ear as she was face down on the hotel bed.

"I'm sorry, babe. I dozed off," Katie slurred back. "Are you OK?"

"Yeah, I'm OK. I was worried about you. It's almost midnight and I haven't heard a word from you since you left this morning. I nearly called the police."

Katie snapped out of her daze. "No. Don't you be doing that. I'm fine. I was just tired from the drive. I spoke to Jenny and she wasn't very nice to me, so I got a bit emotional and came to the hotel. Then the journey must have finally caught up with me and I fell asleep. Nothing sinister." Katie fought to make her voice as even as possible. "I'm sorry, babe."

There was a pause. "OK then. I'd better leave you to sleep. But call me in the morning, OK? Promise?"

"I promise. I love you, Tom."

"I love you too. Night."

Chapter 15

AFTER A RESTLESS NIGHT, Katie showered and dressed roboti-
cally, her mind in turmoil. She only had one place to go on
her to do list today and, after skipping the complimentary
breakfast and checking out of the hotel, she headed straight to
her car.

Pam's little blue Nissan was parked up on her drive when
she passed it, but Katie wasn't here to see her today. She
carried on past her childhood home, so as not to attract Pam's
attention again, hoping that Pam hadn't got that much of a
good memory these days for unfamiliar looking Renault Clios
prowling along the quiet, leafy road. Katie pulled up three
houses down and got out of her car. As inconspicuous as she
could be, she slid up the driveway and disappeared around the
back of her old home, which appeared to be unoccupied. A
for sale board at the corner of the front garden was clearly not
gaining any interest and the house had been left to wither in
the winters that had passed since any life had been present
there.

She walked along the side of the derelict building but still
definitive memories weren't triggered. Gliding her hand along
the top of the splintery fence, she let the feathery tops of the

overgrown weeds that lined the perimeter run through her fingers.

The back garden was long, grassy, and widened out at the bottom where it also dipped at quite a gradient. There, as if no time had passed at all, was the cabin shed that filled the whole of the last 100 feet square of the overgrown garden. As she walked closer, she could see the windows were now cracked and broken at the edges, the putty holding them in their frames crusted and worn. The wood was dark and lichen-covered, with rough circular holes where the knots had once been. The felt on the roof was ripped along the edges, and one end had completely folded back on itself. It was a wreck, barely standing, but the most morbidly intriguing thing Katie had ever laid her eyes on.

In her mind, she started to see hazy pictures of faces she couldn't put names to. The story told to her by Pam and Bill started to play out, as if actors had walked out of the wings and across the stage in her head and begun their performance. She stood motionless, a yard away from the steps leading up to the front door of the cabin, looking up at the imposing structure. Haunted and cold, the building seemed to look back at her, through soulless window-framed eyes. As if mirroring her emotions, the sky began to darken, the clouds above her swirling into grey, edgeless shapes. Air pressure had started to build, and the first drop of rain splashed onto the back of her jacket collar, trickling its way down her neck and chilling her spine.

"What happened here, Mollie? Help me to remember," she breathed into the air.

Once around the back of the cabin, Katie felt the slope descend underneath her feet, and with the rain now falling freely, it began to give way, making traction beneath her trainers almost impossible. She slipped and skidded until she managed to reach out and grab the bottom of one of the decking banisters. Recovering herself, she looked down at the spot where she guessed Mollie may have landed. Katie couldn't stop the tears from falling now, the grim reality of the event she had no memory of. She sank to her knees and pressed her palm flat to the cold, wet earth.

Her thoughts were deafening. *I can only hope you can forgive me. It must have been an accident. You must have been so scared. I hope you didn't feel any pain. I'm sorry I didn't get help straight away. I promise you, if I had my time again, I would do nothing but protect you. I just needed to be here. I need to work out what I do about this now. I'm so sorry, Mollie. I'm so sorry.*

Katie leaned back against the muddy footing of the cabin and made no effort to stop the tears streaming down her face. They mixed with the rain that was now lashing down. By the time she heaved herself up from the sodden earth, she was soaked to the skin. The clouds were starting to separate and a beam of bright sun shone down on her, warming her icy cold, wet face. She trudged back around to the front of the house and down the driveway to her car twenty yards down the street. With nothing else to stick around for, she started the engine and tapped in the post-code to Brighton.

———

SIX HOURS LATER, after hitting every traffic jam on every motorway she drove along, she put her key in her front door and stepped through into the hallway, feeling as if her stiff and weary legs would give way at any point.

"Thank God you're home. I've been worried sick," Tom exclaimed, rushing over to her and wrapping her in a tight embrace. He pulled away and frowned, noticing her white long-sleeved t-shirt was covered in dark mud and bloodstains. "What the hell?"

"Not now, Tom. I'm exhausted. I just want a shower and my bed."

"No, you need to tell me what the fuck is going on." He led her carefully to the living room and sat her down on the sofa. "You can tell me anything, you know that. What happened up in Liverpool to get you in this state?"

"You really want to know?"

"Yes!"

"I'm a murderer."

———

Tom stood staring vacantly at a patch of chipped green paint on the kitchen wall as he stirred a third teaspoon of sugar into his coffee. He snapped out of his daze as Katie appeared behind him, now showered and dressed in a blue wool jumper and jeans. She leaned on the doorframe.

"You *did* ask," she said.

Tom turned around to face her. "How the hell could I know *that* was going to be the story? Never for the life of me did I think you were going to say all of that." His face was ashen, his normally kind eyes cloudy. "All the time we've known each other, you never mentioned anything about that."

"Of course I didn't. Did you not hear the part where I told you I didn't have a clue myself?" Katie replied wide-eyed.

"I know, I know," Tom said, shaking his head. He raked his hands through his thick, brown hair. "It's just a shock, you know?" He checked himself after a sharp look from Katie. "Yeah, yeah, of course you know. Well, it explains why your sister is the way she is with you. She's known all this time and never told you. That's messed up, that."

"It was for my own good, apparently. Though I'm not sure what genius thought that up? Like I was never going to find out?"

"And you can't remember a single thing about that day?" Tom quizzed.

Katie shook her head. Tom's brow furrowed. Katie shot him an angry glare. "What?"

"It's just…just quite a big event in your life for you not to remember a thing about it," Tom replied.

"Don't you think I know that? And how the hell can I go back to work now? With the job I do?" Katie's eyes filled with tears again for what felt like the millionth time.

"Maybe just take a few days off. Say it's compassionate leave or something? Dawn will understand, with it being just after the funeral and all." He looked down at Katie's forearms, now covered with her long-sleeved wool jumper. "And they will need some time to heal too. You can't go showing people them. They'll think you're losing it."

"Are you serious, Tom? I can't ever go back there again. What part of 'I'm a murderer' did you not hear? I killed a child and you think I can go back to work at a *nursery*? Are you out of your fucking mind?" Katie snapped.

Tom rushed over to comfort her. "No, I didn't mean it like that. I just meant… Look, why don't I make an appointment for you at the doctor? You can talk it over with them. It was twenty years ago, and the police didn't prosecute, so you're not in any trouble. And you're not a…murderer. Your sister died, and they put it down to an accident. But you were barely seven years old. How could you know what you were doing? Maybe the doctor can refer you for bereavement counselling?"

"Doctor? So you think I'm fucking nuts now?" Katie wrenched her arms away from Tom's grasp, wincing as she did so. She stormed over to the stairs and disappeared up them, slamming the bedroom door behind her. Tom blew his cheeks out and stood in the almost darkness of the kitchen trying to process what his girlfriend had told him.

———

THE MORNING LIGHT streamed through the blinds in the bedroom window. Katie squinted her eyes and lifted the duvet over her head. A gentle tap on the door made her look. The door opened and Tom's face appeared. He pushed the door open and stood there with a tray of tea and toast.

"I'm sorry," he said, laying the tray on the bed and sitting down. He reached over to stroke her hair.

"Where did you sleep?" Katie mumbled, still half asleep.

"Spare room. I didn't want to disturb you. I checked on you before I went to bed and you were well out. Must have been exhausted." Tom stroked Katie's hair.

"I was. Thanks for this," She reached over and picked up a piece of toast, nibbling the corner. "I'm sorry too. I missed you being next to me. I woke up at 5 a.m. and texted Dawn to tell her I wasn't coming in for a few days."

"Was she OK about it?" Tom replied, taking a piece of toast and munching on it.

"Yeah. To be honest, she wasn't surprised. She said she knew I hadn't been myself, and with seeing Jenny again, she'd sussed out that I felt up the wall with it all. I didn't tell her the truth, though, funny enough."

"We need to take some time to decide how we tackle that part, don't we?"

Katie nodded and looked at him through tired eyes.

"Just let me look after you, OK? No arguments. You've been through hell, physically and emotionally. You need some time to heal. Process it all." Tom kissed Katie's forehead.

"I know."

"Just promise me you won't do that to yourself again." He nodded down to her arms.

"OK."

"Right, I'd better get to work. Those boat engines won't fix themselves." He kissed Katie on the head again. "I'll get us a takeaway on the way home for tea. OK?"

"See you later."

"Love you."

"Love you too."

———

Tom returned home from work to find the house exactly how he'd left it. No lunch plates cluttering up the kitchen sink, the sofa cushions hadn't been crushed under the weight of someone sitting on them, and the TV remote hadn't moved from its position on the arm of his favourite chair. He cast his glance upward and heard no signs of life. Panicking, he raced up the stairs, taking two at a time, and burst into the bedroom, dreading what he might find. There, to his relief, he saw Katie, sitting on the edge of the bed. Next to her was her overnight bag, packed yet again and ready to go.

"What the hell?" He stared at Katie, who stared back.

"I'm going back up to Liverpool."

Chapter 16

"MORNING, BOSS," Mags said as she walked past Rachel at the bike rack in the police station car park. Rachel looked up from her combination lock and breathed in Mags' perfume.

"Oooh, that smells nice. What is it?"

"La Vie Est Belle, by Lancôme. Chip buys it for me from the duty free every time he goes away on a golfing trip. Probably so I let him go. He doesn't know I secretly love the peace, so don't tell him." Mags grinned. "Did you have a nice evening?"

"Yeah, thanks. Just a quiet one."

"Our young DC is doing well, isn't she? Putting us all to shame."

Rachel smiled. "She's a promising talent, that one."

A glint appeared in Mags' eyes. "She's definitely ambitious. Sharp by name, sharp by nature."

Rachel frowned. "That's good, isn't it?"

Mags narrowed her eyes and leaned into Rachel. "Some people don't care who they climb over to get to the top. Chloe might come across as butter wouldn't melt, but just be careful with that young lady." She gave Rachel a slight nod before walking into the police station.

"Excuse me, do you work here?" a voice piped up behind Rachel.

She turned around to meet the tired eyes of a young dark-haired woman wearing a blue wool jumper and jeans. She looked like she had slept in the clothes she was wearing, Rachel deduced, from the creases in her jumper. Her ponytail was askew, leaving wispy brown strands untied in it. Down the right side of the woman's cheek there were two fine red lines the width of a seatbelt apart.

"I'm Detective Inspector Rachel Morrison. Can I help you?"

"My name is Katie Spencer. I've killed someone."

———

RACHEL AND DC CHLOE SHARP observed Katie through the one-way mirror into the interview room where Rachel had asked her to wait. She was sitting straight-backed in an uncomfortable wooden chair behind the table, wringing her hands and staring at the door.

"Is that really what she said?" Chloe asked. Her eyes were wide with incredulity.

"Yep," Rachel replied. "Came straight out with it. Driven up here from Brighton. Set off at 4 a.m." She turned to look at Chloe. "Right then, I can't wait any longer for Mags to get off the phone. Let's you and me do this."

They entered the room and sat down opposite Katie, who was sitting still, her hands now clasped together on the top of the table, which was fixed to the ground. She was looking, through unseeing eyes, down at the laminated card of instructions stuck to the tabletop. Hearing the door open, she lifted her eyes to meet Chloe's curious blue-eyed gaze. Chloe put a machine coffee down in front of her.

"Here you go. Black, no sugar, right?"

Katie murmured her thanks and took a sip from the coffee.

"Right, Miss Spencer—" Rachel began.

"Please. Katie's fine."

A loud, irritating beep sounded as the recording machine went through the startup process, and when that had finished, a small light on the control panel began to blink, indicating that everything was working properly.

Chloe nodded to Rachel, letting her know she could begin.

"Katie, this interview is going to be tape recorded. My name is DI Rachel Morrison, and the other officer present is DC Chloe Sharp. At the conclusion of the interview, I'll explain how you can obtain a copy of the recording, but the short version is that if you are subsequently charged with an offence, you or your solicitor will automatically be provided with a copy."

Katie nodded, looking worried.

"Katie. You're not under arrest and are free to leave at any point. You are also entitled to free and independent legal representation while you're here. Before we started, you told us that you did not want a solicitor present. However, if you change your mind for any reason at any stage of the interview, please tell us and we will stop the interview at once and arrange for one to be provided. Do you understand?"

"I do," Katie said, "but I don't want a solicitor. I just want to get this off my chest."

"Very well. You said something very serious to me outside and I'd like to talk about it with you. Before I do, I must caution you. That is, you do not have to say anything, but it may harm your defence if you fail to mention something that you later rely on in court, and anything you do say may be used in evidence. Do you understand that?"

"Yes, I do," Katie said quietly and took a deep breath.

Chloe leaned forward and watched her carefully, her pen poised over her notebook.

"For the purpose of the tape, will you repeat what you told me outside, please, Katie?" Rachel said.

"Like I said to you outside, I recently found out that I am

responsible for my younger sister's death. It happened over twenty years ago, when I was seven. My older sister knew all about it, as did the rest of my hometown. But I was never told the extent of what happened. For some reason I must have blocked it out completely. I was sent to live with my aunt in Brighton and from then until now I was living a normal life. But my aunt died a few weeks ago, and at the funeral my older sister was there with her five-year-old daughter, Charlotte. The next day I went to see them, as I want to try and get to know my niece, you know? And reconnect with Jenny, hopefully. That's my older sister, by the way. I wanted to feel like I have some family left. But while I was there, I found out about a child called Mollie. I asked Jenny and she wouldn't tell me, so I decided to come up here and dig around in my childhood area. I spoke to my old next door neighbour, Mrs. Parker, who knows everything, and one of my dad's friends and, well, I found out everything. Mollie was my five-year-old younger sister. A sister I couldn't even remember having, until a few days ago."

Katie paused to take another deep breath.

"What happened the day Mollie died, Katie?" Rachel asked, leaning forward and interlocking her fingers on the surface of the table.

"They told me I'd had an argument with Mollie and I pushed her off the balcony of a cabin shed thing we had in the back garden of the old house. She fell about ten feet, onto some rocks below, cracking her neck on the corner of the steps. I went there the other day and saw where it happened. She died instantly, I was told."

"Who told you, Katie? How do you know all of this is true?"

"My neighbour. She told me it was a massive story at the time. That the news and press were crawling all over the street when it happened. And my dad's best friend, Bill Thompson, remembers being there that day. The day it happened. He saw it happen."

Rachel looked at Katie, a sympathetic smile on her face. She got up and laid a hand on Chloe's shoulder. "I'll be back in a minute, Katie, OK?" Katie nodded.

"For the purposes of the tape, DI Morrison is leaving the room," Chloe said as the door closed behind Rachel.

———

Katie sat with Chloe's eyes fixed on her. "Bet you think I'm a right crank, turning up here with a story like that, don't you?"

"No, of course not. I can imagine you must be really confused by all of this," Chloe said. "And it's not for me to judge you anyway. We just want to get the facts to see if there's a case to investigate. Why did you come all the way up here today? Why not a police station in Brighton?"

"I'm not sure. But it just seemed like the right thing to do. I came back up to try and piece together this whole mystery. It's not every day you find out you're responsible for killing someone you didn't even know existed, is it?"

"You're right on that one."

———

Rachel returned to the interview room and sat down.

"For the purposes of the tape, DI Morrison has reentered the room," Chloe said in a well-trained, clear voice. Rachel nodded at her and resumed the interview.

"Katie, I've just checked on the police crime database and for the dates you stated, there is nothing that mentions you by name to have committed this offence. It has the story of a young girl, named Mollie Spencer, at the address you gave, being found dead, but it was ruled as a tragic accident, and an accidental death was logged by the coroner and the pathologist at the post mortem. It was decided by the police that no further action would be taken." Rachel sat back and spread her hands. "I don't know if this puts your mind at rest or not, but there's nothing else to be said on the matter. Officially." She smiled. "I hope that helps you?"

Chloe closed her notebook and stretched out a finger to stop the recording.

Katie looked at Rachel. "Helps? How the hell can it help me? So I 'accidentally' killed Mollie? My poor little sister. It doesn't matter how it happened. I'm still responsible for a death."

"Morally, maybe? But legally, no. You're free to go, Katie. But if it's something that's unresolved with you, maybe you could go and see someone to talk it through?"

Katie leaned forward and licked her lips. "Can I ask…the investigation into Mollie's death? Was it *properly* investigated? Statements, witnesses. Were they properly taken and recorded?"

Rachel's eyebrows knitted together. "Why do you ask?"

Chloe gave Rachel a sidelong look.

"I was just wondering who was spoken to. Who gave witness statements?"

"Well," Rachel began. "If it had been *my* investigation, I would have interviewed anyone who was present that day, who saw what happened."

Katie gave a dry laugh. "It would be interesting to read my dad's version of events. He sent me away not long after, so I'm told. I don't suppose there's any way I could read what he——."

Rachel bristled. "No. You know I can't let that happen. Confidentiality and all that."

Katie looked down at the table. "I guess. I just have so many gaps in my knowledge. I guess I was just hoping for some understanding of the whole thing. I'm sorry."

"Don't worry. Look, here's my card." Rachel fished into her jacket pocket and passed a business card to Katie. "Call me if you find out anything else that concerns you, OK? DC Sharp here will see you out." They all stood up and walked out of the interview room.

AT THE EXIT, Chloe whispered to Katie, "Will you be OK?"

"I'll have to be, won't I?" Katie replied with a stoic look. She straightened her back and smiled. "It's my own stupid fault asking my sister about that bloody photo. Sometimes ignorance is bliss, right?"

Chloe nodded. "Well, as DI Morrison said, if you find out any more information, let us know. Take care, OK?"

"Thank you. I'm sorry to have wasted your time."

Chapter 17

A WEEK PASSED between Katie sitting in the police interview room and the waiting room she was now sitting in back in Brighton. Secretly, she had searched online for the names of hypnotherapists, hoping that in some way they could take her back to that fateful day. Finally finding one, she had booked an appointment and was now waiting for her turn. She answered her name, called by the receptionist and was now sitting opposite a well-dressed, middle-aged man holding a clipboard against his crossed knee. He had sandy brown hair, large brown eyes and a neatly trimmed stubble beard. He wore grey, well-tailored suit trousers, a crisp white shirt and a purple-edged grey wool jumper. After making his preliminary notes, he looked up and gave Katie a soft look.

"So, Katie. What brings you here today?"

Katie fiddled with the cuff of her jacket. "Um. I don't even know where to start. It's all such a jumbled mess."

The hypnotherapist smiled. "Let's try from the beginning, shall we?"

Katie took him at his word. "I read on your website that you offer regression therapy. Is that right?" She looked at him through unblinking eyes.

"That's right. Only if the client is willing to fully open up, though. It doesn't work otherwise."

"Can you take me back to my childhood?"

"We can certainly try." He leaned forward in his black leather tub chair and laid his clipboard on the small side table next to him. "But I want to make it clear from the outset that in the first session we don't always get results." He rolled his hand over and over. "It's like unlocking your subconscious to an extent where you take away the blocks in the memory. It is an ongoing process, even affecting you after you leave here. Your brain will still go through stages of understanding and processing what you've recalled."

Katie listened as the hypnotherapist continued to explain. "Is it scary?"

"It all depends what you want me to help you remember." He spread his hands. "I don't know what's in your childhood yet, do I?"

Katie's eyes filled with tears. "Nor do I."

———

DC Chloe Sharp slid her tray along the counter in the police station canteen, flashing a bored, indecisive look at the lack of options on the pass. Finally choosing the Monday special, shepherd's pie, she grabbed a juice box and sauntered over to the cashier. Just as she was paying for her lunch, she noticed Rachel sat at the far end of the canteen scrolling through her phone. Seeing nothing on the table in front of her boss, Chloe reached back to the chiller and picked up a second juice box.

"Here, you look like you need it," Chloe said, placing the juice box in front of Rachel and sitting down opposite her.

Rachel looked up from her phone. Her eyes crossed for a moment while she refocused them on Chloe. "Cheers." She looked down at the juice box and, seeing it was her favourite orange juice, gave Chloe an appreciative smile. "You really do remember every little detail about a person, don't you?"

Chloe felt her cheeks redden as she tucked into her limp looking pie. "No bad thing. You OK?" she asked, diverting the conversation away from herself.

Rachel let out a long, deep sigh and popped the straw into her juice box. "Yeah, just trying to make some headway on this latest case. I've gone through all the digital case notes and spent most of the morning in archives. But the filing in this place is shit." She took a long drink and sat back in her chair, fiddling with the straw.

Chloe chewed slowly and twirled the fork around her plate, her stare not lifting from Rachel. "You can only do your best."

Rachel looked at Chloe with mock severity. "I get measured by my hit rate. And it doesn't help when everything I need is not in the right folders."

Chloe gave a wry smile. "I guess Mags isn't the best person old Jenkins could have put in charge of archive filing, is she? I'd have put everything on a database by now."

Rachel let out a deep, frustrated groan. "I swear they've brought me up here just to fail."

———

KATIE SAT in the same black leather tub chair she'd sat in a week earlier, her face set in an unenthusiastic grimace. It had been forty minutes since she'd arrived, and the hypnotherapist had tried all the soothing words he could think of. He paused, checked his watch and asked Katie to open her eyes. She met his brown-eyed stare and shook her head.

"I'm sorry to be glum, it's just I'm worried. Nothing's happening again, like last time. I'm trying to delve deep in my memory bank, but nothing is standing out to me."

The hypnotherapist clasped his hands on his knee and smiled. "It can take time. I told you that last session. Don't put too much pressure on yourself. Do you want to stop? I won't charge you for this session if you want to give it some time before we try again."

Katie clenched her teeth in determination and laid her head back. Her hands gripped the ends of the armrests. "No. I want to try again."

The hypnotherapist pressed the play button on his music player and the therapy music gently washed over the air in the room.

———

"I come bearing gifts. Thought you could do with an evening on the hard stuff," Chloe said, holding up a bottle of freshly squeezed orange juice. Rachel held her front door open and stepped to the side to let her in, taking the bottle from her.

"Tropicana. The finest vintage, I see," Rachel said. "You're spoiling me now, Chloe."

"Well, it is Friday night. Let's go wild," Chloe replied, a mock manic grin on her subtly made up face. She was out of her usual well-tailored trouser suit and wearing casual blue jeans and a pink wool sweater. She took her converse trainers off by the door and stepped into Rachel's living room. "Finally got unpacked, then?" she remarked, noticing that Rachel had put her books on the shelves and a few family photographs on her oak sideboard.

"Yeah," Rachel called back from the kitchen down the hallway. She returned moments later with two wine glasses filled with orange juice.

"Nice touch," Chloe said, clinking glasses with Rachel. "How's it going with Adam?" She nodded over to a picture of Rachel with a dark curly-haired man about the same age as her. They were sitting on a bench in a park, with Buckingham Palace in the distance behind them. The smiles on their faces took Rachel's mind back to happier times. She looked inward for a moment, then back at Chloe, the sadness in her eyes thinly veiled.

"A little bit of progress yesterday. He actually replied to a text. First time in, ooh, I don't know how long." Rachel took a long drink from her glass.

"Yeah?"

"Yeah." Rachel smacked her lips. "Small steps. Anyway, what's the latest with that Tinder guy?"

Chloe sat down on the sofa and sipped her juice. "Didn't bother meeting him in the end."

Rachel's eyes swiveled. "Why? You were raving about him last week. What changed?"

"Nothing. I just didn't fancy it in the end." Chloe's tone had an edge to it that made Rachel's ears prick up. Ever one for noticing body language change, she watched Chloe carefully as she took a seat on the sofa next to her.

"You should give Johnny Bradley a chance. He seems a nice guy. Underneath all that aftershave, that is," Rachel joked. "He thinks you're quite a catch."

"Oh, what is it with everyone in that office trying to match me up with every guy that walks by?" Chloe blurted out. Rachel recoiled and held her hands up. Before she could apologise, Chloe beat her to it. "Sorry. It's just…well, I get that from Mags as well."

"Don't apologise. It's your personal life. You can see who you want to see. Or not see."

They both laughed, and the awkwardness between them melted away.

"What do you think of Mags?" Rachel asked. "Honestly."

Chloe made a face. "On or off the record?"

"Off, of course. You're off the clock now, Chloe."

"Ditzy, lazy and a pain in the arse, actually. Oh, we all pretend to get on with her, and she comes across as everyone's mum. But we all know she's just biding her time until she can cash in her pension and sod off to Brazil. I guess she was a good copper once but she's lost the love for it now. Spends more time showing us holiday photos and making us jealous." Chloe took a big intake of breath at the end of her rant.

"Wow, don't hold back there, will you, Chloe. Feel better?" Rachel said, smiling.

"Sorry. But you did say to be honest. I know I was brought over to the Task Force to hoover up all Mags' knowledge as part of the handover of duties between us, but I'd much rather just learn from you. Anyway, I wanted to tell you something when I came over here tonight. I have a bit of a confession to make." Chloe ran a fingertip around the top of her glass. "You know the Spencer case?"

Rachel sat up "Yeah, but we're not looking into that one, though." She raised a stern eyebrow.

"Officially, no. But I have a mate down in archives and I got curious."

"I'm not going to like what you're about to tell me, am I?" Rachel said with a grimace. "How many paid police hours have you spent in archives with your pal?"

"None. I went in on the weekend. You want to know what I found out, or what?" Chloe said with a glint in her eye.

"Go on, then."

"Well, I took a closer look at the Spencer file and there was a medical report tucked in the back of it. I almost missed it until it fell out when I was putting the file back on the shelf. There's a reason why Katie can't remember anything about the day her sister died. She was drugged afterwards."

Rachel recoiled. "Drugged?"

"Yeah." Chloe sat up in her seat. "You see, she was given medication after the incident, to basically remove her short-term memory. She had therapy afterwards to insert false memories of that time, the idea being to fill the gap in her timeline and in effect protect Katie from the horrific reality of what had happened. They knew they couldn't help Mollie, but Katie still had a chance of a normal childhood if they could stop her remembering. It was a really controversial plan at the time and had never been done before. But the doctors thought they had nothing to lose by trying. They decided the stigma of being a child killer was worse for Katie than any side effects or downsides of the medication. This way, Katie wouldn't suffer with any PTSD and would hopefully make a valuable contribution to society. It was all in the case notes and the medical report. You could argue that the experiment worked. She remembered nothing and just got on with her life."

"I'm not sure Katie would appreciate the idea of being a lab rat, though, regardless." Rachel said. "What was the drug they gave her?"

"Can't remember off the top of my head. It had a really long name. Not used anymore, though, for obvious reasons and because of the side effects."

"Which are?"

"Well, the main one is, and Katie probably won't even know it, but it makes female test subjects infertile."

Rachel closed her eyes. "Bloody hell."

"I know. The medication was deemed as a trial. And it hasn't been done since. Social workers and other health professionals deemed it too unethical, so it was the only case of its kind." Chloe smiled hopefully at Rachel. "So you're not mad at me for digging into this case, then?"

Rachel looked impressed. "Not at all. It shows diligence. Aptitude. And I can hardly be mad with you researching the case on your own time, now, can I?" She fixed her stare on Chloe more intently. "Are you looking for promotion or something?"

"What do you mean?"

"I mean, you're great at what you do. I wouldn't want it to go to waste. Have you thought of going up through the ranks and applying to take the sergeants exam next time around? I know it would take months of study to learn the syllabus, and it's a bloody hard exam, believe me, I remember. But I reckon you're more than capable. I'd provide you a written statement of support if you decide to go for it. It's the least you deserve after these last few weeks of hard work and ingenuity."

Chloe tilted her head, as if weighing up that idea, but shook her head. "Of course I've thought of it. But I'm really enjoying what I'm doing at the moment. And who I'm working with," she added, focusing her eyes on Rachel. "Getting promoted too fast would get in the way of gaining valuable experience, so there's no rush at the moment. I want to learn from the best."

———

Katie returned to a house pitched in complete darkness. Apart from his work boots on the mat inside, there was no sign of Tom. She took off her jacket, hung it up and walked into the kitchen where the light clicked on and made her jump.

"Where have you been? I've been leaving you messages." Tom was sitting at the kitchen table wearing a concerned yet quietly angry expression. His voice matched his composure.

"I already told you in my text earlier. I went to Lauren's."

Tom shook his head and clenched his mouth. His hand raked through his messy brown hair. Katie didn't notice, turning to the sink to fill the kettle.

"She's having trouble with her boyfriend, so asked me to come round for a drink and moan. You know how she is. Tea?" Katie asked.

Tom stared at her back. Finally, he spoke through tight lips. "Did you give her money?"

Katie spun around, still holding the kettle while the tap gushed out freezing cold water. "What? No. Why would I give her money?"

"I checked our latest bank statement earlier."

"Why?"

Tom bristled and leaned forward across the table towards her. "Remember us discussing the other night about me needing some new tools for work? After we'd decided together that I should get them, I checked to see if we had enough in the joint account. We have. Just. But the account is

£150 down." His statements were short but loaded. "I know I didn't take it out. So, what did you need all that money for? Money we can't afford to shell out without good reason. I was going to call the bank, because I thought your card had been cloned or something. Until I noticed that it had been drawn out in three separate chunks of £50. What's going on, Kate?"

Katie let her body rest against the kitchen counter. She put the kettle down. "I was going to put it back as soon as I got paid," she said, her voice even so as not to agitate Tom even more.

Tom stood up and set his face. "I'm only going to ask you this once, Kate." He puffed out his chest. "Are you seeing someone else?"

Katie rushed over to him. "Of course not, babe. Why would you draw that conclusion?"

"Because you took a lot of money from our account without telling me. We don't do secrets, Katie. We always said that. Why couldn't you tell me what you needed that money for?" He pushed her cloying arms away from wrapping themselves around his waist.

"It's just something I needed to do. I didn't tell you because I was afraid of what you'd think," Katie said, trying not to cry.

"And *this* reaction is better?" he replied, his eyes like saucers. "Bearing in mind I don't get paid when I ask to finish early to support you while you've been feeling down lately. You know how tight money is for us at the moment. Dawn will probably only give you full pay for so long being off. We are lucky she is as nice as she is."

"I know." Katie sank her face into her hands and began to sob.

Tom placed his hands on her shoulders. "Tell me what that money has paid for the last three weeks?"

Katie looked up at him, her eyes red, her face puffy. "You promise you won't get angry if I tell you?" Tom gestured to hasten her explanation. "I've been going to see a hypnotherapist."

Tom took a step backwards.

"Why?"

"I want to remember what happened all those years ago. To Mollie. It's breaking me apart not being able to recall what happened. I don't understand it and I needed help. I wanted to be regressed."

Tom was speechless. After a moment he licked his lips and tried to keep his voice as even as possible, all the while shaking his head to try and understand what she'd told him. "You want to be *reminded* about killing your five-year-old sister? Quite possibly the worst incident that could ever happen to a person. An incident your brain has blocked you from ever remembering? And you *want* to remember it? Are you sick in the head or something?"

"I need to know what happened, Tom."

"Why?" Tom yelled, waving his hands at her.

"Because. I can't explain why. I just do."

They had reached an impasse. They stood toe-to-toe, staring wide-eyed at each other, red-faced and exhausted. Tom shook his head and pinched the bridge of his nose. "OK, OK. But please tell me, after a hundred and fifty quid's worth of talking, this magical fucking therapist has helped you find the answers to your burning questions?"

Katie looked down at her trainers. "Not exactly, no. Not yet. It takes time, he said."

"Fucking great!" Tom exclaimed, walking past her and over to the kitchen doorway. "How much time?" He walked back over to her and cupped her chin in his shaking hand. "Katie, how much is this going to cost us?"

"I don't know. But I have to do this. Please. Try to understand."

"I'd understand more if you paid for therapy to *deal* with this past of yours, rather than to dig it all up again. What do you want? To visualise what you did? To feel it all over again?

You must see how damaging that would be? It's sick, babe. You need to let it go. For your own sake, as well as ours."

"I can't drop it. I owe it to Mollie to find out the truth. Maybe I deserve to feel it. I know the police didn't prosecute me for what happened, but maybe I should be made to feel the consequences of what I did. I want to see what she looked like. Jenny has a photo but she won't let me see it. It's like Mollie never existed. Never lived. I need to find a way to understand it all."

Tom breathed out a long, angry sigh and softened his shoulders. He looked at her, his angry eyes now soft. "Look, babe. What happened was tragic. It really was. But it's in the past. And it needs to stay there. No good can come of raking it all up. Don't you see that? Knowledge isn't always a good thing to have. What's the saying? Ignorance is bliss? I think that's true here. You said yourself the police deemed it an accident. And if they think that then clearly you did nothing wrong. All this stress on you is not going to do you any good. Not to mention it messing about with your hormones. We've got a future to plan for, babe. Our own family. Our own kids. We can't be looking back in the past."

Katie looked up at him, her eyes still glistening with tears. "You still want kids with me? Even though you know what I am? What I did?"

"Of course I do. You were a child yourself. You didn't know what you were doing. It was twenty odd years ago. Like I said, it's all in the past. We need to look forward." He scooped her face into his broad hands. "I love you."

Katie sniffed and wiped her nose on her sleeve. "I love you too."

"Just promise me all this hypno-crap will end now."

Katie pressed her face into his shoulder, muffling her reply just enough.

———

Tom found Katie an hour later in the spare room making up the bed.

"You sleeping in here again tonight?" he asked her, his face downcast. He picked up a pillowcase and fiddled with the cotton seam.

"Yeah. I just thought with everything going around in my head that I probably wouldn't sleep very well. And you have to be up at five."

"I could lie with you until you go to sleep, then get my head down?"

Katie walked around the bed to hug him. "I'll be fine. Honestly." As Tom turned to leave, Katie's phone beeped. Looking down at her phone, she smiled.

"Who's that?" Tom asked.

"Oh, just Dawn." Katie read from her phone. "She's asking how I am and if I'm taking it easy. Says they're looking forward to me coming back, but to take my time."

"You need to take her advice," Tom said with a wry smile.

"She says in her message too that when I'm ready she'll help me with my assignment. That's if I even carry on with that course now. Either way, I am lucky to have a boss like Dawn."

"They see what I do. How special you are. You've put years into that nursery, even before you started your course when you were volunteering, and they know that. Plus you're never off sick, so Dawn knows it's important for you to take this time for yourself."

Katie's eyes looked inwards for a moment. "It was always my dream to run that nursery one day. Even start up my own. That's blown to shit now." She hugged the pillow she was holding close to her chest before laying it on the bed and patting it into shape.

"You still can. Nothing has changed, babe."

Katie looked up at him. "Nothing's changed? How can you say that? Can you imagine if people found out I'm a child killer? Even saying those words out loud makes me want to be sick. How in the hell would any mother want me looking after her kids when they found that out?"

"Look, just don't make any big decisions tonight. You've had a long day. Sleep on it. Please?" Tom's eyes implored her.

"I can't escape the feeling that there's only one thing for it," Katie replied.

"What?"

"Resign."

<hr>

Tom crept back into the spare room, a whimpering coming from Katie waking him up. He padded over to the bed and silently sat down, reaching over to gently wake her. "Shh, shh, it's OK, babe," he said, gently stroking her clammy forehead. But her writhing became more violent as her nightmare appeared to get worse. Starting to panic, Tom grabbed her forearms and held her tightly. "Babe, wake up. Katie, wake up," he shouted. With a jerk, she came out of her nightmare, her eyes wide. Tom pulled her into him and stroked her sweaty, matted hair. "It's OK, just a bad dream."

"Shoes!" Katie blurted out, pushing him away from her. Tom looked at her in complete confusion.

"What?"

"Shoes. I saw a pair of shoes," Katie repeated, as if saying it twice made it make sense.

"What shoes? Where?"

"Where Mollie died. I saw a little pair of shoes at the top of the cabin's steps, just outside the door. But they couldn't have been mine, Jenny's or Mollie's shoes," Katie shrieked.

"How do you know?" Tom stared at her intently.

"Because they were little boys' shoes."

Chapter 18

Maggie Chapman held her morning coffee cup close to her chest as she gazed out of her kitchen window at the perfectly manicured back garden. At the far end were weeping willow trees, in full bloom and cascading their long tendrils down towards the lush green lawn. Rose bushes bordered each fence of the Chapmans' large detached bungalow, which spread itself over almost an acre on the edge of Formby near the beach. Behind her a rattle of metal sounded, breaking her out of her daydream.

"Sorry I didn't make it home last night, darling. You know what the nineteenth hole can get like on a Sunday night," a deep, lightly scouse-accented voice purred behind her.

Mags turned around to see her husband Patrick, known as Chip to everyone who knew him, standing in the kitchen doorway. He was in his late fifties, tall and spare with thinning blond hair and a closely trimmed stubble beard. He was wearing a typical golf enthusiast's attire: beige slacks with deep pockets, a navy pullover shirt with collar and short sleeves, and a white baseball cap which he now held in his hand. His keen blue eyes were fixed on his wife's reactions to him being out all night. Next to him were his golf clubs, standing proudly in their top of the range black and white

Dunlop golf bag. They shone in the morning sunbeams that danced across the marble effect polished floor tiles, all the way to Mags' slipper-covered feet.

"That's alright, Chip. But I'd appreciate a phone call next time. Good round?"

Chip grinned and folded his tanned, hairy arms. "Yeah. Really good. I shaved another stroke off my score. Frank wasn't happy." He flashed a wicked smile and poured himself a coffee from the pot Mags had made. "How was work?"

Mags exhaled. "Same old, same old. I can't wait until we're sailing around South America on our yacht. It's just not the same there anymore. Too many tech-savvy whippersnappers making dinosaurs like me feel inept."

"Just a few more months, darling. Then we're selling up and out of here for good." He lowered his lips to kiss her on the cheek. "I'm going for a shower." He checked his Breitling wristwatch. "You'd better be getting to work."

———

RACHEL PULLED her bike up on the rack near the police station car park seconds after seeing Mags walk past and towards the entrance to the building. She clinked the combination lock into place and took her helmet off, feeling her pocket vibrate as she walked over to the entrance to the station. It was a text from her mum. Quickly, Rachel tapped a reply saying that it wasn't a good time for her to come up to visit her, then hesitated as she pressed the send, knowing that the usual lecture about not taking it easy and working too hard was bound to follow.

Inside the incident room, Rachel saw that Tina Saunders was walking around each desk holding a tin of something she'd no doubt baked the previous evening. As she walked over to her office, Rachel almost crashed into the tin as Tina held it out to her.

"I made some scones. And there's custard creams in the

tin over by the kettle. Can't have us running low on essentials now, can we?"

Rachel smiled and declined a fruit scone that was thrust in her face. She turned around and bumped into another cloying presence.

"Phone call for you, boss," Mags said.

"Who is it?"

"She wouldn't say. But she sounded agitated and insisted on speaking only to you. Mentioned you'd spoken to her a few weeks ago?"

"OK, put her through." Rachel walked into her office and picked up the phone. "Detective Inspector Morrison speaking."

"Is that Rachel?" the voice on the line replied.

"Yes. Who's this?" Rachel said, taking out her notebook just in case.

"Katie Spencer. The woman who was a mess outside the police station that time. You helped me."

"Oh, of course. I remember. You sound upset. Are you OK?"

"You know my case?"

"Yes."

"I've remembered another detail. There was someone else there the day my sister died."

"Right. OK." Rachel jotted down what Katie was saying, then nibbled on the end of her pencil. "Do you know who?"

"No. Can you tell me, please, were any other children spoken to that day? Other than me and Jenny?" There was a pause. "It's important."

"Katie, how has all of this only just come to light?" Rachel said, switching phone hands. She heard a deep exhale through the phone.

"OK, I know this sounds crazy, but please believe me but…I've been seeing a hypnotherapist recently who has tried regression therapy on me, and even though the sessions didn't show me much of the events of that horrible day when Mollie died, I had a dream last night and remembered something. One detail my brain finally unlocked."

"What did you see?"

"I saw the scene, Rachel. Well, part of it. It was all still pretty hazy. But I feel that each time I think about the dream, I unlock another piece of the scene. That's why I'm ringing you to ask if there were any other children questioned that day when Mollie died. Because of the shoes I saw in my dream. They were at the top of the cabin shed steps, just outside the door. Dad and his friend Bill would never allow you inside the cabin shed if you had muddy shoes on, and it had been raining that morning so…"

"Are you sure they weren't yours? Or your sister's? You said yourself you have lots of gaps in your memory. How do you know for sure you or your sister didn't own them?"

"Because they were *boys'* shoes," Katie replied, her voice cracking.

"I see." Rachel noted it down. "And you don't have any brothers or cousins who were visiting?"

"No."

It was Rachel's turn to leave a pregnant pause on the line. "Katie, all of this was looked into back then. All evidence would have been bagged and tagged. I'm sure the police would have followed all procedures and everyone would have been spoken to who needed to be."

"Please, Rachel. I need to know. Just tell me if a boy was interviewed. That's all I want to know. Please."

Rachel held a hand up in surrender. "OK, OK. I'll see what I can find out. But, Katie, if you want my advice, you really need to try and find a way to move on from this."

"You wouldn't be saying that if it was you, believe me."

The line went quiet. Rachel thought on that for a moment. "I'll do my best for you, Katie. Take care."

Chloe appeared at the door holding a mug of coffee just as Rachel put the phone down. She placed the mug in front of her.

"Everything OK?" Chloe asked.

"Yeah." Rachel's misty eyes became keen. "Could you do me a favour?"

Chloe's face lit up. "Sure…what do you need?"

"Can you bring me the witness reports from the Spencer case file, please? I need to see if a child, a boy, was ever interviewed at the time."

"I'll get right on to it," Chloe replied, turning to go.

Rachel smiled her thanks and lifted the cup to take a thirsty swig. Before the cup touched her lips, she thought of something else. "Actually, can you bring me the whole file? I need to see that medical report. Specifically, the bit about the use of drugs on Katie to help her forget what happened."

———

As soon as she'd put the phone down to Rachel, Katie made another call. The voice that answered, on the tenth ring, sounded breathy and irritated.

"Hi. Jenny. It's me. Katie."

There was a pause. Katie heard Jenny clear her throat. "What do you want?" Jenny replied.

"Look, I know you don't like talking about this, but it's been on my mind since I found out. The day Mollie died, do you ever remember seeing another kid there at the house? Did we have a friend, a neighbour's kid, hanging around? A boy?"

"What? Why are you asking me this? Look, I'm not being funny, Katie, but I get that you might want to rake all of this up again, but I don't. Why can't you respect that?" Jenny's voice became more hard-edged, with every word in her final sentence punctuated like punches to Katie's face. Nevertheless, Katie carried on.

"It's important, Jenny. I'm sorry it hurts you, but I need you to remember."

Jenny exhaled at length. "When I got over there, there wasn't anyone else hanging around, no. I've got to go now."

"No, wait," Katie said. "I saw some shoes. At the top of the cabin shed steps. Whose were they?"

"What do you mean, you 'saw'?"

"I had a dream last night. You see, since I found out about Mollie, I've been having regression therapy with a hypnotherapist down here. I think I've started to unlock—"

"Now, you listen here," Jenny snapped. "I wouldn't wish the sight of what Mollie looked like that day on my worst enemy. The fact that you actively *want* to see it is beyond sick. What the hell is wrong with you, Katie? They were right to keep this from you. Look at how you're acting about it now? Look, if you're having difficulty coping with what you now know you did, then yes, get therapy for it. But only a person sick in the head would want to be taken back to that time. You're making the past the present. For both of us. That's unfair, Katie, and I won't be a part of it. I take pills to *forget* what happened and to help me sleep, so forgive me if I don't want to chit-chat about remembering that day in detail."

Katie could sense Jenny was about to hang up. "I just think there's more to it than what we both know—"

Jenny let out a bark of laughter which echoed loudly down the line. "Oh, so that's it? You want to pin it on someone else. You've lived the last twenty years of your life guilt free, while others had to live with what you'd done, and even now you think you're entitled to flick it off your shoulder like a lump of dandruff? You are so fucking selfish, Katie. I cannot believe this."

"No, not at all. I just think… I don't know what I think. I just feel there is more to this story. And if, at the end of all this, I am the one who was solely responsible, then I will live with it. But someone else was there, I know that now. They might have seen something no one else did. The only witnesses to what I am supposed to have done are Dad and Bill Thompson. But when I spoke to Bill—"

"You spoke to Bill? When?"

"When I came up to Liverpool. I came to see you, but you

weren't in when I got there, so I got curious and went to visit the old house while I waited. It was the day I saw Pam Parker. Afterwards I went to speak to Bill. I had so many questions that even he couldn't answer. And I can't speak to Dad for obvious reasons, and you don't know anything else. Please, Jenny, try to understand."

Jenny laughed. "I'm really trying to stay polite here, Katie, but the audacity of what you've done is unbelievable. Just because *you* want answers to what *you* did and what *you* can't remember, you want to put everybody else through an ordeal they have spent twenty years trying to forget. You think *I* didn't have counselling for what happened? I did. I still have dreams. Nightmares. I have to *unwillingly* live with the memories that you have chosen to unlock. And now you want everyone else to compromise their sanity to make you feel better?"

"No, I didn't mean for anyone to have to feel it all over again for themselves. I just wanted to know if you remember anyone else being there that day. I don't want you to have to see the aftermath of Mollie's fall, or death, or…"

"The only person we ever knew in that street that was around our age was a lad called Robbie. Robbie Reynolds. Lived up the road. He used to do a few odd jobs around the backyard for Dad. Just for a couple of quid to help him and his family out as they were skint and scruffy. They were sick of him hanging around the house bored, so it got him out of their hair for a while. His mum was ill and his dad didn't have much time for him, really. When Dad and Bill were doing some repairs on the cabin shed, they asked Robbie to help lumping wood around for them and collecting up the nails that fell down between the decking boards."

"Do you think Robbie could have been there that day? Were they his shoes at the top of the steps?" Katie's eyes were wide, her words firing out of her mouth as quickly as they'd shot across her brain.

"Probably. Wait a minute, are you suggesting Robbie killed

Mollie? That's pretty fucking twisted, Katie. Even for you. Dad and Bill saw you standing over Mollie, looking down at her broken, dead body from the balcony you pushed her from. Robbie was a nice lad, wouldn't harm a fly. No one else did it, Katie. It was you. *You* need to face up to that."

"All I'm asking is… Look, thank you for telling me about Robbie. I'll go back to the police and ask if Robbie was spoken to. And if he wasn't, maybe I could go and speak to him. Can you remember if his parents still live in our old street?"

"Are you for fucking real? You've dragged me into it and now you're going to drag them into it too? Listen, Katie. Listen very carefully, because I am so fucking done with this, and you. Fuck off. OK? I don't want to hear about this anymore. Just fuck off."

"Jenny, please—"

Three beeps sounded, and the phone went dead. Katie screamed into the silent air and threw her phone down.

Chapter 19

"WE'RE all upstairs ready for your Wednesday briefing, boss," Mags said, appearing behind Rachel who was sitting at a small table in the archives room surrounded by cardboard boxes and files. Rachel looked up at her, then down at her watch.

"Christ, is that the time? Thanks, Mags. I'll be up in a sec."

"How long you been down here for?" Mags said, wrinkling her nose at the stale air in the small area Rachel was working in. It was lit only by an insufficient strip light above them. "You'll strain your eyes trying to read in this light."

"Since seven. I wanted to make an early start."

Mags' smile faded from her face. "I thought we were a team?"

"Huh?" Rachel looked up to see Mags had now folded her arms and was stern faced.

"You're keeping a lot to yourself lately. Doing the jobs that I should be doing. You're meant to delegate, you know."

Rachel took her reading glasses off and pinched the bridge of her nose. "It's no reflection on you, or your ability, Mags," she said, in as genuine a voice as she could fake. "It's more of an 'it's bugging me' kind of thing with a case I'm looking into. Not official police work."

Mags pursed her lips. "Is it a case we're working on at the moment?"

"No, not exactly. I just want to make sure I've given some-body the right information about something." Rachel gave Mags a nod of dismissal, then looked back down at her case folder. Mags remained standing in the doorway. She put her hands in her beige summer jacket pockets and exhaled.

"Right, I'm just going to come right out and say it," Mags said. Rachel looked up to meet her steely glare. "With respect, ma'am, I know my time here is almost up, but I'm still a copper. I still care. I may be clumsy, and I may be forgetful, but I'm still a detective at this station. And my thirty years' experience should entitle me a modicum of respect around here. So, please, don't cut me out of cases. I know DC Sharp is the new bright young thing around here, and being trained up to replace me, but I have something still left to offer the team too."

Rachel looked at her, softer this time. "Look, I'm really sorry if you feel left out, Mags. I guess I can be a little stub-born in cases. Too independent, that's what my mother always says. Always trying to do it all myself."

"You don't seem to have any difficulty asking Chloe Sharp for assistance," Mags said in a quiet voice.

"I see it as giving her experience," Rachel replied with a diplomatic smile.

"Fine. As long as you don't forget *my* experience," Mags riposted.

"Noted. But on this one," she pointed down at the case file she was reading, "I just need to satisfy a curiosity I have with a strange case I'm following. Then, once I'm back on our cases, then I will take into account what you've said and split the labour more according to rank *and* previous experience. OK?"

Mags' hard exterior melted. She let a wide smile drape across her round face. "Perfect. Coffee?"

"Thanks. Now, let's get to this briefing."

———

THE BRIEFING LASTED HALF AN HOUR, and afterwards Rachel took a walk around the perimeter of the police station. The stale air of the archive room had given her a headache and the sunny late morning freshness outside was too tempting to resist. Plus, the change of scene would do her mind good. It had been turning over and over since she'd started looking into the Spencer case. What looked like an open and shut case, two clear-minded witnesses and a child who been caught in the act, now seemed to have a few unanswered questions linked to it. If Katie had seen a pair of boys' shoes, whose were they? The case report would make interesting reading. The problem was that it was an old file relating to an accidental death. Retention rules for non-suspicious deaths weren't as strict as those for murder enquiries and she was actually quite surprised that any of the paperwork had survived this long; in most places it would have been destroyed by now. As she strolled, Rachel found herself wondering just how thorough the investigation had been. If Mollie's death had been viewed as accidental from the get-go, the investigating officers might not have gone to the same lengths that they would have had they been investigating a murder. It was frustrating to think that she might not find the answers she sought, even after reading the case file. Still, Rachel's copper's nose was itching.

As she turned the last corner of the building, her phone rang in her pocket. "Morrison."

"DI Morrison? It's Katie Spencer. I need to talk to you."

"Katie, hi. Are you OK?"

"Robbie Reynolds," Katie blurted out. "He's the boy who might have been there that day Mollie died. They might have been his shoes."

"Oh, right."

"Can you check the report to see if that name is in there? If Robbie was questioned?"

"I can look over the statements when I get back to my office. If he was, would that put your mind at rest?"

"Yes. I'd have to accept what I did and get over it." Katie paused. "Somehow."

"And if he wasn't?"

Katie's voice hardened. "Then I'll need to find him, wherever he is now, and ask him what he remembers. I know you won't reopen the case, so I'll have to do it on my own. I need to know. I can't think of myself as a killer. It just doesn't feel right."

"Katie, look," Rachel began, trying to choose her words diplomatically. "I didn't want to have to tell you this. But…"

"What?"

"I was hoping it would all be left, and I guess I wanted to protect you from finding this out but…" Rachel paused as two police officers walked past her and into the building. A gust of wind blew a long strand of hair across her eyes, adding further seconds to her pause.

"What?" Katie said louder.

"Well, I do have some information regarding your case. The long and short of it is that because of your age at the time of the incident, taking into account the traumatic nature of the experience and the possible impact on you and your development through the rest of your childhood—"

Katie let out an impatient growl to get Rachel to cut to the chase.

"A decision was made to put you through therapy, and on a course of medication to help you forget the whole thing."

"What?" Katie said. "Was that even legal?"

"It was legal at the time, yes. Probably not now. But whether it was ethical is a subjective decision. The fact was that Mollie was dead, and nothing anyone could do could change that. But the doctor that assessed you afterwards, well, their intention was to try and make sure your mental health wouldn't suffer. Try and avoid two tragedies. It was controversial, though, as the drugs they gave you were very strong. They never used them again, mainly because of the side effects." Rachel stopped talking when she noticed Katie was now distant on the line. "Are you still there?"

"What were the side effects?" Katie asked in a thin voice.

Rachel took a deep breath. Normally she wouldn't allow herself to be drawn this deep into a disclosure of confidential information, but she knew there was no way Katie would let the matter go now. "I'm sorry to tell you, but it's highly likely you'll never be able to conceive."

There was a gasp. Then a cry. Then the line went quiet.

"Katie? Are you there? Do you have anyone with you right now?" Rachel suddenly realised the safeguarding issue of telling a twenty-seven-year-old woman over two hundred miles away that any future family plans were effectively ruined. "Is your boyfriend home?" The three beeps she heard indicated the call was over.

———

Katie shrank to the floor and curled up in a ball. Clutching her phone in one hand, her other covered her mouth.

"Katie, are you OK? I heard a thud." Tom appeared in the bedroom doorway still holding the TV remote. "Why are you on the floor?" He looked down at Katie perplexed as to why she was lying next to the bed, not on it.

"Oh Tom, I'm so sorry. I've destroyed everything. It's all my fault." Katie broke into deep, hacking sobs that triggered Tom to launch himself over to her to wrap his arms around her shaking shoulders.

"What the hell's happened? Calm down. Please." He held her tightly into his body and tried to get her to breathe with him. Finally, she was calm enough to speak.

"Not only did I apparently kill my sister, but I've killed our future too. It's all my fault why we can't have a baby, Tom. I'm so sorry."

"What? How? I don't understand." Tom looked down to see her phone screen still lit up from the last call she'd had. "Who were you talking to before I came in? The doctor?" He sat back and stared at her.

"No, the policewoman I met up in Liverpool. She told me some more details about my case. I can't remember what happened to Mollie because they made me take medication to forget. It was basically a fucking medical trial. I was a fucking guinea pig. Until they realised it had side effects. It made me infertile, Tom. And there's nothing I can do about it now."

All of the colour drained from Tom's face as Katie's devastated sobs had a second wave.

Katie wiped her face with her hand and set her lips hard. "It's my own fault, I guess. Penance. I did a horrible, evil act. It's only right I be punished. I took a life, so I should have life taken away from me." She looked at Tom. "I can't expect you to stay with me now. I'll understand if you want to leave. I wouldn't blame you." She creased into tears again. "Oh, God, Tom, I'm so sorry. You were so looking forward to having a family, and I've fucked it up."

He sat for a moment trying to gather his thoughts. He reached over for her and pulled her into his lap, cradling her head. "Don't be ridiculous. I'm not leaving you. Not ever. I don't care if we can't have a baby naturally. There are loads of ways we can make that happen. But the most important thing is that we get you calm." He kissed the top of her head and rocked her.

"I don't deserve you," Katie said, her soaking wet face buried in his t-shirt. Just then, her phone rang again. It was Dawn. Katie sniffed and wiped her face. "Hi, Dawn," she said, trying to sound as composed as possible as Tom held her weight in his arms.

"Katie? Umm… Are you able to come into work tomorrow?" Dawn's voice paused on the line. "It's urgent. We've had a call."

Katie dropped the phone.

———

"So, no one by the name of Robbie Reynolds was ever spoken to by the SIO on the Spencer case twenty years ago?" Rachel said, looking up from the case file on her desk and taking off her reading glasses. She slid the file over to Chloe who was seated across from her.

Chloe scanned through the file and shook her head. "Nothing mentioned in any of the statements about a boy being present. Or anywhere near the house, to be honest. No shoes found at the scene either."

Rachel tutted and leaned back in her chair. "She insists she saw a pair of boys' shoes."

Chloe made a face. "Maybe she's delusional? She's relying on a memory that manifested itself in a dream, triggered by a regression. Hardly a strong basis for proof, is it?"

Rachel nodded. "Hardly surprising her mind is in tatters, though. Being told your sister is dead because of you must be shattering. Passing the blame to someone else, I guess, is the only hope she has of living with it. In some ways, I get it."

"Me too. I'd probably do the same," Chloe said.

"Can you look this Reynolds boy up, Sharp? Just so I can box it off."

Chloe recoiled in surprise. "Really? Off the back of what she said?"

Rachel tapped her nose. "When this itches, I can't ignore it. Believe me, it's served me well in the past."

Chapter 20

"Off anywhere nice?" Supt. Jenkins asked as he read over the form Rachel had dropped on his desk early on Thursday morning.

"Scotland. I've worked up enough time to take a day off, so I thought I'd go and tie a few loose ends up on a case I've been looking into."

Jenkins paused before signing at the bottom. "If it's a case you're working on, then you don't have to take a day's holiday for it."

Rachel shook her head. "It's an old case, yes. But a closed one. I think there's more to this one, though, so I need to be sure before I let it go. Your budget is stretched enough without me costing you money in pay and expenses."

Jenkins chuckled. "That's why we like you here, Morrison. Your frugality. We'll make a northerner of you yet." He put his pen to paper. "Which case?"

"The Mollie Spencer case." Jenkins was blank faced. "Twenty years ago, five-year-old Mollie Spencer was killed by her seven-year-old sister, Katie. But I think there are holes in the investigation, so I'm trying to help the family get some closure on it. Namely, Katie herself. She's adamant she didn't do it."

Jenkins looked up. "Wasn't that case signed off as an accident?" He fixed her with an inquisitive stare. "How come you're looking into it?"

"Because I'm not convinced it was an accident," Rachel replied.

———

Katie stood outside Dawn's office, the letter of resignation she'd typed out last night tightly clenched in her hand. She lifted her free hand to knock just as Dawn opened the door.

"Katie, hi. Come in," Dawn said in a somber voice. She was wearing a black trouser suit and pink blouse. She took her seat behind her desk and waited for Katie to sit before fixing her with a long, strangely cold look. "As I said to you on the phone, we've had a call. Look, there's no easy way to say this but…"

She paused. Katie's fingers gripped the letter. Taking a deep breath, Dawn continued. "Ofsted have decided to come and inspect tomorrow." Dawn's expression changed from grave concern to hope. "I need you back here, Katie. I know that's ridiculously selfish of me, what with you going through hell right now. But I can't get through this inspection without my star player. Please? Say you'll stay today and help me prepare, and come in tomorrow while they're traumatising me?" Her eyes were wide and pleading.

Katie crumpled up the letter into the palm of her hand and surreptitiously slipped it into her pocket. Sighing inwardly with relief, she smiled. "Of course I will, Dawn. Just tell me what you need me to do."

"Can you go through all the public liability insurance documents, and make sure the health and safety certificate is all up to date? I'm pretty sure it's due for renewal, so I need you to make sure that's sorted. Between us we can sort out the resources and brief the rest of the staff. Will that be OK?"

"Of course," Katie replied.

Tom walked into the bedroom after a long day at the boat-yard. Taking off his dirty jeans and t-shirt, he threw them into the laundry basket as Katie rolled over in bed. Her face was streaked with dry tears and lined from the chequered pattern on the pillow.

"How did it go with Dawn?" Tom asked, sitting on the edge of the bed.

"It wasn't what I thought. The call was from Ofsted. She just needed me to come in to help her prepare for the inspection tomorrow."

"Oh, right. OK. You heard anything back from that copper yet?"

Katie shook her head. "I bet she doesn't take it seriously. I'm just a crank to her, probably. Making more work for her."

"Well, they are the ones with all the power to look into it. I guess what will be, will be."

Katie sat up and hugged the duvet around her knees. "I don't even know what I'm hoping for."

"For somebody to have a clearer explanation for what happened than your hazy memory can provide, maybe." Tom stroked her head and smiled.

"Could that be worse, though?" Katie replied.

Katie walked into the toilet cubicle at the nursery and slammed the door. She put the lid down on the toilet and sat down with a thump, raking her dark brown hair through her fingers. It had only been an hour since the inspectors had been there, going over each and every page of paperwork, but already she was feeling the strain. She took out her phone and called Tom.

"Love, I'm at work. What's up?" Tom said down the phone.

"I can't cope with this. The lead inspector is an absolute dragon. Not to mention how she looks like Morticia Adams. She's scaring the children." Katie ranted until she ran short of breath.

"You rang me to slate the woman who has the potential to shut you down and put you out of the job, and off your course?" Tom replied mock seriously.

"Yes. And you are my boyfriend and it's your job to listen to me rant."

"How is it going, really?" Tom asked.

"OK, I suppose. I'll just be glad when it's over. And Morticia goes back to her coffin."

Tom laughed. "Gotta go, love. See you later. Be nice."

"Bye." Katie hung up. She took a huge deep breath and composed herself. Standing up, she opened the cubicle door and walked over to the sink to splash her face. Another cubicle door opened behind her. When she looked up, she found herself standing next to the lead inspector, her expressionless eyes fixed on her. She was wearing a long black dress and suit jacket. Her jet black hair shone in the strip lighting above them, her scarlet lips a thin slit across her slab face.

"Hi. Umm… Have you, umm, got everything you need?" Katie said.

"Yes. Thank you," The inspector replied, her tone monotonous. She nodded and turned towards the exit, leaving Katie to kick herself for her indiscretion.

———

Dawn opened her office door later that afternoon and froze for a second, as the lead inspector stood like an apparition in front of her. "Cynthia. How's it going?"

The lead inspector frowned and opened her red slit mouth. "We have found a problem here. My colleagues and I have discovered something that has raised some serious concerns. We believe that the children here could be put at serious risk."

Dawn swallowed hard and held her arm out to invite the lead inspector into her office.

———

THE DRIVE to Scotland was long, but the scenery Rachel passed once she was over the border was stunning. Heather-covered fields stretched on either side of the M74, only breaking when she reached the small villages that were peppered along the route. The M74 changed to the A74, and each town along it seemed to be a copy of the last, comprised of whitewashed stone terraces and the odd playground by a small, grey stone built primary school across the main road. The town she was looking for was twenty miles to the east of Glasgow, and, as she approached the sign welcoming her to Crailach, she took her foot off the accelerator, slowing her Alfa Romeo to the required thirty miles per hour speed limit.

Green fields filled with freshly shorn sheep flanked both sides of the dirt track she had been directed to follow by an old man with a straggly grey beard who was walking along the road with his red setter dog. After mumbling his answer in his broad native accent, he had pointed and gestured along the track up to a farm Rachel could now see on the horizon. Now approaching it at low speed, she clenched her fingers around the steering wheel as she drove over a cattle grip that rattled all the pens in her dashboard like marbles in a bag. With trepidation, she negotiated the wheels around the dry potholes that she feared her low-suspension car would be wholly unsuitable for tackling.

She reached the front yard of the property and got out of her car. Standing and stretching her legs after her long drive, she scanned the area for signs of life. It didn't appear to be a working farm. The machinery she saw, including an old tractor with no windscreen and a giant rip in its back left tyre, was rusty and bent, as if it had not been used for its purpose for many years. The farmhouse was dull grey stone, with weeds growing all around the foundation stones. The windows were dirty, covered in some kind of green lichen and mostly intact, save for one on the lower left side which had a long, forked crack along the diameter of it. The front door was solid looking oak, painted black at some time in its life, but the paintwork was now chipped and flaking away, not helped by the biting westerly Scottish winds and icy rain. The farm was truly in the middle of nowhere, and apart from the old man she'd passed on the way here, and the fields full of livestock, she hadn't seen another living soul for miles.

"Can I help you, hen?" a small, croaky voice piped up from around the side of the building. An old woman stood peering at her, a quizzical look on her face as she took in the smart-suited, official-looking woman about to knock on her farmhouse door. The old woman was wearing a brown woollen skirt, a navy blue wax jacket and sturdy-looking Wellington boots. Her head was covered with a brown and dark green tartan scarf, revealing a few strands of long, greasy-looking grey hair. Her face was deeply lined and weather-beaten but her sharp blue eyes were keen. She was holding what looked like a makeshift scythe.

"Oh, hello. I'm sorry to bother you. My name is Rachel. I'm looking for Robbie." Rachel, sensing that this farm wasn't used to visitors, decided to leave out her rank and profession from the introduction.

"Why? What's he done?" the old woman replied, stepping forward. She was easily into her eighties, but the gnarled hand that held the scythe still looked strong.

Rachel took a step backwards and flashed a disarming smile. "Oh, nothing. I wanted to have a quick chat about something. He's not in any trouble."

"Nan, who are you talking to?" came another voice from around the farmhouse. Appearing at the old woman's side was a young man, around thirty years old, wearing dirty blue jeans, a navy blue woollen jumper and heavy work boots. His dark brown hair, slightly curly at the temples, was speckled with what looked like sawdust. He looked at Rachel with watchful, brown eyes. "Who's this?" he asked, pointing.

"Hi. Robbie, is it?" Rachel asked, inclining her head towards him. A gust of wind blew a strand of her long brown hair across her eyes, which she wiped away.

"Who wants to know?" the man replied. The old woman jabbed him in the side with a long, bony finger.

"Polus," she said out of the corner of her mouth to the man. She looked at Rachel, a glint in her eye. "I may be old, lassie, but I'm nay stupid. I know a detective when I see one. So what's the story?"

Rachel sucked in her cheeks and took out her warrant card and showed it to the old lady and the young man. "You've got me there. DI Rachel Morrison. And you both are?"

"Morag Brown. This here's ma' grandson, Rab." The old woman pushed the young man forward.

"My name's Robbie." He cast a look over his shoulder. "Nan calls me Rab for short. What can we help you with, detective?" His voice was polite, with a slight scouse twang, but it had picked up the rural Scottish burr his grandma spoke with.

"I'm looking into an old case. I wanted to ask if you knew, or remembered, a girl called Mollie Spencer?"

Robbie's legs seemed to buckle slightly. He reached his hand out to the wall of the farmhouse to steady himself. His stubbly face turned as grey as the stone. "Jesus. I've nay heard that name in a long while." His eyes looked inward for a moment, then he shook his head and stared into the middle distance. "Why are you asking about her after all these years?"

"So you do remember her, then?" Rachel said. She watched his reactions carefully. "Do you remember anything about the events of the day when she died?"

"It was twenty years ago. I thought it had all gone away

now." Robbie still couldn't bring himself to make eye contact with Rachel. He screwed his face up and continued to focus on something way out in the fields across from the farmhouse.

"Like I said, it's an old case we're looking into. Her sister, Katie is," Rachel paused, searching for the right word, "concerned that a few details don't quite fit with her recollection of events. So I was hoping you could tell me what you remember."

Robbie's eyes widened as he fixed Rachel with a hard stare. "What I remember?" He began chewing on a dirty fingernail. "Oh, so *now* you wanna take it seriously?"

Rachel frowned. "Take what seriously?"

"Now, Rab. Calm yer'sel. Nay be takin' it out on the polus lady now," Morag said, her eyes flashing a warning glare at her grandson. She reached out to pull at his sleeve. "Why don't we go inside and have a cuppa wi' the nice wee lady?" She gave Rachel a thin smile.

Robbie wasn't listening. He shrugged his nan's hand off his forearm and jabbed his finger into Rachel's face. "I spoke to you lot. Back when it happened. I spoke to my parents to tell them what I saw. I even told the vicar at our local church because nay person would listen to me. But even he told me to mind my own business and nay get involved. And now you come here, after all these years, pretending you're interested in what I have to say?"

"Yes. I'm very interested, Robbie. Will you talk to *me*?" Rachel's face was set with determination not to be intimidated by Robbie's hostile body language. Her words were soft, her manner relaxed, her experience in these situations obvious. She inclined her head as she remembered something Robbie had said. "Wait. You spoke to the police?"

Robbie backed down, his anger subsiding. He wiped his mouth on his dirty sleeve and began pacing the area. "I went to the police station the day Mollie died. I ran away before the police arrived at the scene because I was so scared about what I'd seen. I was only ten, for fuck's sake. But when I'd calmed down, I knew the right thing to do was to tell someone."

"Who did you speak to, Robbie?"

"Don't remember the name. They didn't take any notes, just said thank you and someone would be in touch. But I never heard anything again. My parents battered me for what I told them when I got home after. They called me a liar and wanted me out of the house. So, I stole mum's address book and a photograph of Nanny Morag and came up here to find her. She agreed to let me stay. Said she could use a strong lad to help her on the farm. Grandad had died the year before I came up here. Fell off the tractor." He nodded towards the battered tractor Rachel had seen when she first arrived.

"Robbie, I'm sorry no one listened to you back then. But I'm listening now," Rachel said, her stare burning with sincerity into Robbie's screwed-up face. "What did you see? The day Mollie died, what did you see?"

Robbie was unmoved. He set his face hard and rose up to his full six-foot height, his fists clenched by his sides. In his eyes was a cold look of disappointment and disgust. "You lot weren't interested then, so why the fuck should I go through all of that again just to help you now?" He set his lips into a thin, long hard line. "Now, unless you're planning to arrest me, or my nan, get the fuck off our farm and leave me alone." He turned and slung an arm around Morag, leading the bewildered old lady back around the side of the house and out of Rachel's sight.

Rachel walked back to her car, her mind turning with the oddness of Robbie's words and behaviour. As she got back in her car and drove back down the lane away from the farm, her phone beeped, having finally picked up a reception. She pulled over and saw it was a voicemail from her mum. She called her number back but got the answer machine.

"Hi, Mum, it's Rachel. Look, I'm up in Scotland on business, but I'll call you when I get back. We'll arrange something for next weekend, yeah? I'll book your train ticket to come up to Liverpool. Have a think about what time is best for you. Talk later, love you."

She hung up the phone and made another call straight after, mindful of the dodgy signal between her location and the nearest built-up area.

"Sharp? It's me. I need you to stop what you're doing and find out who would have been the local vicar in the churches surrounding Mollie Spencer's home address twenty years ago."

"Of course. I'll get onto it now. How are things up there?"

"OK. Robbie lives with his nan, who's an interesting character."

"I wonder if he's told his nan what happened?" Chloe mused.

"Whatever he was saying, people clearly didn't want it becoming public knowledge."

"Could be to do with the plan to keep it from Katie? For her own good, maybe?"

Rachel scratched her nose and wrinkled her face. "No. That all happened afterwards. We need to find out what exactly Robbie saw, and why there is no record of him even being spoken to, let alone what he said."

"Are you heading back to Liverpool now, or staying over?" Chloe asked.

"Straight back. Unless Robbie wants to speak to me, there's nothing up here to investigate further. I'm going to go and take a look at the Spencers' old property too, on the way back to HQ. Have a nose around that cabin shed, just to build a picture of it in my mind."

"Make sure you stop off at services if you get tired and need a break."

Rachel smiled. "Yes, *boss*."

———

WHEN RACHEL RETURNED to the station, ACC Clifford and Supt. Jenkins were waiting for her in her office. It was well after six o'clock and Rachel was exhausted.

"Hello, Rachel. DC Sharp mentioned you'd decided to come straight back from your little trip," Clifford said, flashing a bright white smile.

"Yeah, I was going to leave it until Monday, but I received new information that couldn't wait."

Jenkins looked at her. "New information on the Spencer case? From where?"

"A witness, actually, sir." Rachel dropped her handbag onto her desk and unpacked her notebook and phone.

Jenkins put his hands on his hips. "A witness all the way up in Scotland? By the name of…?"

"Robbie. Reynolds."

Jenkins looked at Clifford, whose dark features creased. "Why has he only just spoken up now? Isn't this case twenty years old?"

Rachel chose her words carefully, uncertain as to the full reason herself. "He said he spoke to a few people back at the time of Mollie Spencer's death. But no one took him seriously for some reason, so he gave up."

"Maybe he was lying and no one believed him?" Jenkins said.

"No, I don't think so. He spoke to his vicar as well as the police and his parents. He said he saw what happened that day but ran because he was so scared. You know as well as I do, an eyewitness is worth following up with."

"Rachel," Clifford said at length. "I understand your diligence, and I appreciate it. It's why I brought you up here in the first place. But when you are using my resources, such as DC Chapman and DC Sharp, and driving from one country to another—albeit on your own time—it becomes my business. Remember, I have to justify where I spend my budget." He paused and looked at Jenkins for a moment, then back at Rachel. "We have open cases coming out of our ears, so I cannot have you traipsing around on ten-hour round trips to interview witnesses to closed cases. Do I make myself clear?"

Rachel swallowed hard. "Yes, sir," she answered as brightly as she could. "But what if I look into the Spencer case in my own time?"

Clifford thought on it and nodded. "I can't stop you, I suppose, if it's in your own time. But I want results on the cases I'm actually paying you to solve, understand?" His deep voice was firm, but fair.

Chapter 21

TOM RACED up the stairs and into the bedroom, thudding down on the bed next to Katie. She stirred awake and sat up rubbing her eyes. "What's going on?" she mumbled.

Tom stared at her and thrust the Monday morning newspaper into her face. "Look. Page four."

Katie thumbed through the newspaper and there it was. Her heart flipped. "Oh fuck. I didn't think they'd do that," she gasped. "Am I mentioned by name anywhere?"

"No, luckily. It's just basic information—location, facts, etc.… Some hack writing a speculative story, no doubt fed by a leak in the police. You've never mentioned having a sister called Mollie, so there's no reason why anyone we know would think you were involved. But if that journalist is right, and people from the area start to put two and two together, it'll be all over the national news by teatime." He wiped his hand across the air. "'Mollie Spencer case reopened', it'll say. Babe, how could you let this happen?"

Katie dropped the newspaper into her lap and buried her face in her hands. "Who the hell would have leaked the story to the police? And why now?"

"Who knows? The story mentions that 'new information has come to light', but it doesn't say from who."

"I'll call Rachel." Katie leaned across the bed to get her phone.

"No, don't. You need to leave this alone now, Kate. Let it blow over," Tom said. Katie put her phone down and read the article properly.

———

KATIE LEFT home for work that morning with her head clouded from the newspaper article she'd read. Finding a note on her desk from Dawn, she headed over to her office. She knocked and entered to find the look on her boss's face the same as when she'd last been in her office.

"Good morning, Katie. Sit down," Dawn said. She was wearing a dark navy business suit and purple blouse with a white and purple chiffon scarf tied loosely around her thin neck. "Well, there's no easy way of saying this, but what I read this morning has seriously concerned me. Katie, you've not only let me down, but you've let the children down, and everyone else who works here. I can't even begin to tell you how disappointed I am." Dawn shook her head and looked as if she was stifling tears. Katie suddenly wished she still had her resignation letter.

"What is it, Dawn?"

"I received the report from the Ofsted lead inspector. Everything was good except for one thing. Katie, you've put the children in serious danger, do you realise that?"

Katie felt her heart thud. Her stomach flipped over. She swallowed to stop herself from throwing up. "Oh, my God, Dawn. I am so sorry. I wish I'd told you sooner what I did. But I just didn't know how to say it."

Dawn's voice softened. "You could have just told me. We've been friends for how long now? You have never let me down before. But this? I don't know how to get over this mistake. The only saving grace is that the health and safety certificate hasn't expired yet. We've got until midnight tonight to get it updated, and renew the public liability insurance, and I managed to finally sweet talk Cynthia Lawton into giving us the benefit of the time window. But Katie, if you didn't get chance to do it, then I would have preferred you to tell me."

Dawn's words were a blur. Then Katie remembered. She was all ready to press submit after filling in the health and safety form when Rachel had called her with an update. She'd left her computer and completely forgotten the form.

"Oh, Dawn, I'm so sorry. I'll get it sorted; I promise." She looked at Dawn, but her face was still fixed in a disappointed expression, one Katie couldn't ever remember seeing on her in all the years she'd known Dawn. It cut her to the bone.

Chloe appeared behind Rachel sitting in the canteen early Monday morning and placed a photocopy of page four of the Daily Star down on the table. Rachel turned to see her with a slight smile on her face. "So, apparently *someone* gave the press an anonymous tip-off over the weekend," Chloe said, tongue firmly in cheek. Rachel put down her bacon sandwich and perused the article.

"I wonder who could have done that," Rachel replied.

"I don't know. Probably someone wanting to get the press hungry for a scandal? Maybe it was someone who'd just returned from speaking to a previously unknown witness, perhaps? So the case would get the green light to be reopened, especially now as there's mention of 'new information'. I mean, I'm just guessing here." Chloe's twinkling eyes fixed on Rachel's.

"No comment," Rachel said with a crease at the corner of her lips.

"How did you get on when you visited the Spencer property? Did you see the cabin shed?"

"Yeah. Hell of a fall from that height. Poor kid wouldn't have stood a chance hitting that rock underneath." Rachel secured the lid on her coffee and stood up. "Right, Sharp. Looks like we've got work to do."

———

"How the fuck could you be so stupid?" Jenny raged down the phone. Katie held it away from her ear, waiting for the initial tidal wave of anger to subside. "Pam Parker's just rung me. It's all over the Star. Have you given a tip-off to a tabloid rag?"

Horrified, Katie gasped. "No, of course not. It was nothing to do with me. I swear. I didn't even know the paper was going to run a story."

"It's really suiting you, all of this 'I can't remember shit' bollocks, isn't it? Well, these things have consequences, Katie. I just hope you don't live to regret what the press know now. It won't be long before they put a name to the killer. And you'll deserve all you get. You've had twenty years of not having to live with the knowledge of what you did. Well, now you get to reap what you sow."

Jenny rang off, leaving Katie to sit at her kitchen table in stunned shock.

———

Sat at the table in Rachel's office, Chloe was beavering away, highlighting key lines in a photocopied version of the Spencer case file, including the medical report.

"OK. So, apparently, after it was ruled as an accidental death, a kind of strategy meeting was held. But only a few professionals attended. There was a psychiatrist, a police officer and a social worker to determine what to do with Katie in the best interests of all involved."

Rachel looked over the top of her coffee cup at Chloe. "Any names?"

"Yep. The psychiatrist and the social worker are named.

No mention of which police officer was present, though. But I guess it would have been the SIO on the case, right?"

"More than likely. But how many DIs have walked through the hallways of Merseyside Police over the years, eh? God knows where they'd be now. OK, give me what you have." Rachel waited for Chloe to write down the names and pass them over to her.

"Oh, and here's the name of the reverend at the church nearest to the Spencer residence. He's still there now," Chloe said, passing over scrap of paper.

"Thanks, Sharp. I'll pop over there this afternoon. See what his take on all of this sad business is."

———

RACHEL PARKED in a small village car park in Allerton and headed down a narrow pathway, bordered by rose bushes, through the lichgate and up to a red brick modern church.

In its grounds were numerous flower beds, bursting with clematis and primrose bushes. There was a small memorial garden with a bench and brass plaques on sticks in the ground. A jumble of old headstones in the graveyard stood at crooked angles as the ground encasing them had subsided over the years.

Rachel walked over to the arched wooden door and into the church entrance. At the far end of the nave, she saw an elderly man with tufts of white hair circling a shiny bald head lighting a sconce of candles in silent prayer. He was wearing a black suit with a white dog collar, it providing the only shard of colour in his sober grey shirt. As Rachel approached him down the scarlet carpeted aisle, he looked up over the top of his half-moon glasses and flashed a saintly smile.

"Can I help you, young lady?" he said in a raspy voice.

"Are you Reverend Carlisle?" Rachel asked.

The vicar put down his lighting taper and clasped his

hands over his middle. "Yes, I am. Call me Clive. I haven't seen you here before."

Rachel reached into her jacket pocket and showed Clive her warrant card. "I did leave a message that I was going to call in this afternoon, but…"

Clive shook his head and smiled again. "It's fine. I've just had a journalist in this morning asking questions about… Never mind. How can I help?" he squinted down at Rachel's warrant card. "Detective Inspector. It must be important if they've sent you." He held his arm out to lead her into his vestry. "Please accept my apologies for being a little put out just then. It's just I've a lot to do. I've got a wedding coming up this weekend, and the rehearsal is tonight so…"

"I won't keep you long. I understand you've been the vicar here since 1998, is that right?"

The vicar chuckled and interlaced his fingers. "Probably longer. There isn't a child in this village I haven't baptised."

"Do you remember a local boy, Robbie Reynolds? He lived on Hancock Street, by the park just across the way there." Rachel pointed out of the vestry window to the main road at the end of the graveyard. "About twenty years ago?"

"Hancock Street, you say?" Clive looked inward for a moment as he searched his memory bank. A few seconds passed before he shook his head. "No. I don't remember a Robbie living there. Is it important?"

"I'm looking into an old case, chasing up some witnesses. When I spoke to Robbie—"

"You spoke to him?" Clive said, looking up from the papers he was shuffling on his desk.

"Yes."

"Which case did you say you were looking into?" Clive asked.

"I didn't."

"The only incident I remember from twenty years ago was…" He broke off and shook his head. "That poor dear child. Dead." He tutted and crossed himself. "God rest her soul. But that was all sorted. Accident, they said."

Rachel nodded. "I'm just dotting i's and crossing t's. You know how it is. Only, there was one thing Robbie said when I spoke to him. He saw what happened and needed to tell someone. He said he spoke to a local vicar after the accident. Did he come to you, or any of your colleagues?" Rachel took out her notebook, hopeful of a name.

"No. No, he didn't. I mean, I can't speak for any of my fellow vicars, but he most definitely didn't come to me."

"How much do you remember about the Spencer case? Did you know the family?"

Clive shook his head. "Not all that well. Peter Spencer, the father, wasn't very religious. I figured it was because his wife died only a few years after Mollie was born. Now I come to think of it, I can't remember him, or the children, ever attending Sunday service. I was asked to conduct little Mollie's funeral, though, but only because the church is so local to them. I hadn't met Mr. Spencer until a few days before the service. He wanted to go over a few details of what he wanted for poor little Mollie." He screwed his lined face into a grimace. "That poor sister of hers, Katie, must have felt terrible about what she did, may God forgive her. Such a tragedy."

Rachel's ears pricked up. "Katie? What leads you to think Katie was involved?"

Clive paused. He licked his papery thin lips and swallowed. "I must have read it in the paper. It was a big story at the time. It was all everyone was talking about."

"I don't remember seeing in the case notes that the papers printed Katie's name." She waited to see his reactions. He thought on what she'd said for a moment, blinking and fumbling with a piece of cloth he'd picked up from his desk.

"Oh, well, you know what small villages are like for gossip. That's what I heard. Now, was there anything else, Detective

Inspector? I'm quite busy and I must get on." He headed to the vestry door and opened it wide.

"Thank you, Reverend Carlisle. I appreciate your time. I'll see myself out." Rachel left the vestry, the door closing behind her. She walked back the length of the church nave and towards the exit.

"Excuse me, dear. Do you know where the Reverend Carlisle is?"

An elderly woman with tightly permed grey hair appeared at Rachel's side. She was wearing a lilac cardigan, beige trousers and a white blouse. A silver and pearl brooch caught the sunlight as Rachel opened the church door.

"He's in the vestry." She smiled at the old lady and turned to leave.

"Thank you." The old lady tottered off down the aisle, her suede loafers padding along the carpet. Rachel had a thought.

"Sorry, excuse me? You might be able to help me."

The old lady turned and walked back to Rachel. "If I can, dear. My name is Joyce Darwin. I'm church warden here. And you are?"

Rachel fished out her warrant card. Joyce fumbled in her pocket for her reading glasses. "Oh, a detective inspector. Why, that's interesting. How can I help with your enquiries?" Joyce stood open-faced, as if she were centre stage in an episode of *Midsomer Murders*.

"Do you remember the Reynolds family? From Hancock Street. Lived there about twenty years back?"

The old lady thought on the question for a few moments. Her light blue eyes lit up as the memory came to her. "Oh, yes. A quiet family. Kept themselves to themselves. Not that religious," Joyce added in a whisper. "But their boy, Robbie, was a lovely young chap. So very helpful. Cute as a button, a head full of brown curls. We had a lot of young boys come through here back then, with the Sunday school. But Robbie was different. Never came to the Sunday school, but was always hanging around doing odd jobs for the vicar. Family was quite poor, so any cash young Robbie could earn used to help them a lot. I tried to give him a little extra when he mowed my lawn. Such a sweet boy." Joyce rambled on as she reminisced. Rachel rolled her hand to move her on quicker. "Every now and again the vicar would send him home with a few tins from the harvest festival baskets. Just to help them along. He couldn't bear the thought of him not having a decent feed. Said he needed some meat on his bones, so he could be fit and strong to help him with the odd jobs around here."

"So the vicar knew Robbie well, then?" Rachel asked, making notes.

Joyce's wrinkly face creased into a wide smile. Her eyes twinkled. "Oh, yes. Robbie was like his shadow. Wherever Reverend Carlisle went, Robbie went. Well, that is, until one day. Robbie just seemed to disappear. We never saw him around the church, or the village, again."

Rachel stood with her pen poised over her notebook. "Mrs. Darwin, when did Robbie disappear? Was it before Mollie Spencer died? Or after?"

Joyce thought on it for what felt like an age. Finally, she prodded the air with her long, bony finger. "After. It was definitely after that dear little Spencer girl died."

Rachel reached out to shake Joyce's hand, which the old lady took heartily. "Thank you, Mrs. Darwin. You've been incredibly helpful."

"You're welcome, dear. Now, was it the vestry you said the reverend was in?"

———

RACHEL RETURNED to her office later that afternoon, Joyce Darwin's words still reverberating around her brain. If she was telling the truth, then that meant Reverend Carlisle was telling lies. But why? She sat with a thud in her office chair and, as if her prayers had been answered, Chloe Sharp appeared holding a cup of freshly brewed coffee.

"I saw how you walked in. Figured you'd need this. Tina's on her way in with her famous ginger cake. Try it, you won't regret it." Chloe's chipper face darkened when she saw Rachel's hadn't moved. "Penny for them?"

"I've just come back from speaking to that vicar. Reckons he's never heard of Robbie Reynolds. But I spoke to the church warden on the way out who told me a completely different story, so…" Rachel spread her hands.

"Which vicar is this?" Tina Saunders said as she walked in holding a tartan-coloured cake tin.

"The one from St Mary's, near Hancock Street in Allerton. Clive Carlisle. You ever come across him on any of your church fundraisers?"

Tina's face clouded over. "I shouldn't really speak ill of a member of the church. It's not very Christian."

"But?" Rachel said, leaning forward.

"Well, I've always had a bit of a bad feeling about him." She hugged the tin close to her chest, her cardigan buttons clanging against the metal. "Outside that church, he has a bit of a reputation. But nobody really discusses it *openly*, if you know what I mean?" She shook her head, as if wishing she'd never mentioned anything. "It's all gossip, really. Cake?" she held out the tin, which Rachel waved away.

"What gossip?" Rachel said, standing up. Before Tina could answer, Mags burst into the office behind her.

"Well, you'll all be pleased to hear that case Bradley and I were working on this week is all boxed off. Mother and daughter are now reunited, hatchet buried and planning a bloody good holiday, so I'm told." She smiled at the faces in the room, looking at them one by one for accolade.

"Well done, Mags. Another one off the list," Rachel said.

"I've asked Johnny to type up the notes now and get it logged as solved on the database. On to the next one then, eh,

Johnny-boy?" Mags called out to Bradley, who was sat at his desk giving Mags a thumbs-up. She swept out of Rachel's office as quickly as she'd swept in, leaving only a waft of Lancôme in her wake. Tina turned to leave also, cake tin still full.

"You OK?" Chloe asked when it was just the two of them left in the office.

Rachel's eyes were unfocused, her thoughts racing. "Hmm?"

"You OK?" Chloe repeated. "You don't seem to be with it, not since you came back from speaking to that vicar."

Rachel took a huge swig from her coffee. "This Mollie Spencer case is really foxing me. I don't know whether I'm opening up a can of worms here. I'm going off the word from an eighty-odd-year-old church warden that the local man of the cloth is telling lies to me. Whose memory do I believe?" He tired brown eyes locked with Chloe's sympathetic ones.

Chloe exhaled and perched on the edge of Rachel's desk. "I was always told to 'follow the evidence'. If something doesn't slot together, or make sense, then there's a reason for it. If I were you, I'd investigate every detail until it made sense. And if it's nothing, at the end of all of this, then at least you can say you did all you could and officially close the case."

Rachel's brow softened. "I'll speak to the social worker who was involved in the meeting about Katie, then the psychiatrist and the police officer, if I can find out who it was and where they are now. At least that might join a few dots."

"Won't Robbie talk to you? Maybe if you tried again? It's been a few days now since you met with him. He might have calmed down."

Rachel shook her head. "No. He despises the police. The look he gave me was pure hate. I don't blame him, really. If he told the police something serious, but they didn't believe him, or follow it up, there's no way he'd have any faith to try that again. Especially as he ran away from home over it."

"Who did he speak to when he came into the station?"

"No record was ever made of him even coming in, let alone the name of the officer he spoke to."

Chloe thought on that for a moment. "I suppose there is a chance Robbie could have lied? Maybe he had more to do with Mollie's death than we thought. Maybe he said he came into the station to cover himself? And when they didn't take him seriously it made him feel he was in the clear? It's all ifs and buts, I guess."

"He could have lied, yes. But so could the police."

"Really?"

"It happens. More than you would think sometimes."

"Why, though? Why would the police cover up the truth about how a little girl died?"

Chapter 22

RACHEL POCKETED her warrant card after introducing herself to the pleasant, open-faced young receptionist of a private therapy practice on Rodney Street. The small waiting room she was now sitting in had off-white-painted walls, a lilac carpet and lilac faux leather tub chairs. There was a small coffee table in the middle of the room, laden with leaflets asking the reader if they had ever considered how amazing the 'inner you' would be if only they could learn to love themselves. Rachel inwardly rolled her eyes and sat patiently while the receptionist rang through to the therapist she had come to speak to.

"You can go in now, Detective Inspector Morrison," the blonde, perfectly made-up receptionist purred through red matte lips.

Rachel rose and walked over to the therapist's door, knocking lightly.

"Come in."

"Hello, Doctor Martin King?" Rachel said after walking in. Sat at a solid-looking dark oak desk was an athletically built man in his early fifties, with black curly hair, a Roman nose and intelligent blue eyes. He was wearing a three-piece steel grey Armani suit with a pink and purple striped tie. The gold tie pin attached to it glinted in the light from the computer screen he was looking at.

"How can I help you, Detective Inspector?" the therapist said, taking off his black-rimmed reading glasses and smiling that familiar therapist's sympathy smile. "Please. Sit." He gestured a thin, well-manicured hand to the lilac-coloured tub chair in front of his desk. The therapy room was similarly decorated, with the theme of serene purples and lilacs running through from the waiting room. In the corner was a giant green and yellow yucca plant underneath a well-covered cork notice board of leaflets, helpline numbers and business card-sized ads. In the other corner there was a long therapy bed with the obligatory sheet of blue roll paper draped over it.

Rachel sat down in the tub chair. "I'm conducting some enquiries into an old case and was hoping you could help shed some light on a few matters."

Doctor King leaned forward and interlaced his fingers on the desk. "Of course. Anything I can do to help you. Please, ask away."

Rachel's eye was caught to the row of accolades that were displayed on the wall in gilt-edged gold frames behind King's head. "You're a sleep specialist, is that correct?" Rachel asked, nodding up to the certificates.

"Yes. Oh, I know what you're thinking." His eyes creased at the corners as he put on a mocking voice. "With a name like Martin King I must get loads of people ringing me saying, 'I had a dream' but, if I'm being honest, it doesn't happen that much." He let out a bark of laughter, which exposed a perfect set of shiny white teeth.

Rachel pressed her lips together. "No, that's not what I was thinking, actually," she said as politely as possible. "I wanted to ask if you remember a strategy meeting that was called twenty years ago where you discussed the case of a Katie Spencer?"

King's broad shoulders stopped rippling as his laugh faded. He composed his face. "I've attended a lot of strategy meetings. And you're asking me to cast my mind back twenty years and remember?"

Rachel stifled a smile. Ironic, she thought, given what he'd done to Katie and her memories.

"Can you elaborate, please?" King asked.

Flipping open her notebook, Rachel found the page where she'd written down her notes about the treatment Katie had been given. "According to the case file we have on Katie Spencer, back in 2000 a social worker, a senior police officer and yourself attended a strategy meeting to discuss the best course of treatment for Katie, who was just seven years old at the time she allegedly killed her younger sister, Mollie. The decision made at the meeting was that Katie should be given a course of treatment and medication prescribed by you in order for her to essentially lose her memory up to and including the incident. She would then undergo an untested false memory therapy, which, according to the meeting notes, was for her benefit. It was designed to replace the horrific nature of the incident and give her the chance of a normal life afterwards. She was then moved out of the area, to avoid triggers from her surroundings, down to the south of England to live with her aunt, so there would be less chance of dangerous flashbacks and/or vigilante attacks, so it was deemed in her best interest." Rachel took a breath and fixed her stare on the therapist, who had listened intently through-out. "Now do you remember the case, Doctor King?"

He nodded. "I do indeed. But like you said, that was twenty years ago. And as far as I know the case was closed. What brings you here after all these years?"

"Could you confirm for me the name of the medication you prescribed, please?"

King thought for a moment. "Eradopram, if I remember correctly. I can check for you if you don't mind me taking a moment to search though the file?" After Rachel nodded her permission, King slipped his glasses back on and tapped away on his computer keyboard, then pressed the return key. "Ah, here we are. Eradopram, fifty milligrams." He swivelled in his chair to face Rachel and looked down his glasses at her. "We don't use it anymore, though."

"Because of the side effects?"

King took his glasses off, slower this time, and laboured over closing the stems. His lips were set in a thoughtful straight line. "Yes. But, on the positive side, we've never had another case like Miss Spencer's where we felt it was in the best interest of the child to recommend this treatment. We wanted to give her a second chance at life."

"Doctor King, before Katie took the medication, did she ever actually *admit* to killing Mollie to anyone? Or in fact having any involvement whatsoever in Mollie's death?" It struck Rachel suddenly; had anyone actually asked that question before? King's jovial, laid-back manner seemed to change. He now sat straight-backed and stony-faced in his high-backed expensive black leather chair.

"It was too long ago for me to remember that."

"I'm sure you kept some kind of patient notes. I mean, what doctor effectively changes a patient's whole life story without jotting down a record of it?" Rachel's stare hardened towards the therapist.

King's eyes narrowed. "Why are you asking me this?"

"I'm curious. Katie Spencer was a seven-year-old child, and before any kind of interview or confession was taken from her, she was medicated and had her memory wiped, on the say so of two supposed witnesses who on closer inspection of their statements made for some contradictions in their reading as to exactly what happened. Can you see now why I'd be curious?"

The therapist bristled. "I'm not a detective. I don't do the interviews. It wasn't my place to interfere with their part of this." His words were floundering as he spread his hands in defence.

"Did you even ask her?"

"No. I was just told the facts of the case as the police saw them. The meeting was for her benefit, to save her from trauma as she got older and to safeguard the public in the hope that Katie didn't repeat what she had done. What I did was to protect her and to protect others."

"Allegedly. What she had *allegedly* done." Rachel tried to keep her voice even, but inside she was raging.

"All procedures were followed. Now, if you'll excuse me, I really need to be getting on." King leaned forward and pushed out his chair to stand up. But Rachel wasn't finished yet.

"Who else was at the strategy meeting? I'd like their names, please."

King sat down heavily and exhaled at length. "There was a social worker that was working Katie's case, Brenda Holroyd. And a police officer…"

Rachel scribbled the social worker's name down and waited with bated breath for the name of the police officer.

"But I don't recall their name," King said, shaking his head. Rachel swore inwardly.

"Right, thank you for your time, Doctor King," Rachel said, standing up. King did the same. "I'll go and pay Ms. Holroyd a visit."

King grimaced. "Unfortunately, you can't. Died. A few years ago, in a car accident." He shrugged.

Rachel fought to contain her frustration. Slinging her handbag over her shoulder, she flashed the therapist with her sharpest glare. "The name of the police officer. Find it in your records and call me." She handed him her business card.

"If you want to speak to me again, Detective Inspector, you will have to do it formally, making an official appointment," King said just as Rachel was about to disappear out of the door. "I might not be able to fit you in as a 'drop in' next time."

Rachel looked at King. "As I am sure you are aware, if it turns out that a crime *has* been committed and you are withholding information, then I'll be *dropping in* with a court order to seize your records. Just keep that in mind, Doctor King."

———

Superintendent Jenkins strode up to Rachel's office and wrenched open the door. Seeing it was empty, he turned around and fixed his impatient fiery glare on Chloe Sharp.

"Sharp. Where's DI Morrison?" he snapped.

Chloe stood up. "Out of the office this afternoon, guv. Can I pass on a message?"

"Tell her my office as soon as she gets back." He stormed off back the way he came.

"Yes, guv," Chloe replied to the swish of air that was left in his wake.

———

"Hi, Mum. Sorry I didn't get back to you straight away. I'm just at work at the moment, but as soon as I get a spare moment, I'll sort that train ticket out for you. OK, bye." Seconds after Rachel hung up, another call came through her hands free. "Sharp. Some good news, please," she said wearily.

"Nope, sorry. Jenkins is on the warpath. Not sure why. Just wanted to give you the heads-up."

"Why does it sound echoey where you are?"

"I'm hiding in the loo. He's in a proper nark. I mean, he's a mizzog at the best of times, but…"

Rachel wrinkled her nose and laughed at Chloe's broad Liverpool accent, which always seemed to come out when she was angry or pissed off. "What's a 'mizzog'?"

"Oh, just some scouse word meaning 'miserable old git', but don't tell him I told you that or he'll have my badge. Are you on your way back?"

"Yeah. On Upper Parliament Street now so I'll be about ten minutes."

"Any luck with the therapist?"

"Not really. I found out the name of the social worker and was going to go over there, but she's dead. It just feels like I'm hitting brick walls all the time. Something doesn't feel right. I don't know, maybe I've lost my edge." Rachel leaned her hands heavily against the steering wheel.

"Don't say things like that. You're amazing at your job. And if you didn't investigate even the most hopeless of cases, then what would be the point of even doing the job, eh? Maybe in some way you feel sorry for Katie and want her to have closure?"

Chloe's rational and soothing words hit a spot in Rachel's brain that calmed her. "Maybe."

"Talking of which, Katie called you for an update just before Jenkins scared me into this smelly bog. She just wanted an update from you, so I told her you'd call her back?"

"Bollocks. I literally have nothing new to tell her. Nothing that will help her, anyway."

"Well, at least you've tried. That's more than any other copper has done for her. Or Robbie Reynolds for that matter. You've spoken to the therapist and can't speak to the social worker for obvious reasons."

"That's not everybody, though, is it? There's still the police officer involved in the strategy meeting. But King was very shady about telling me their name." Rachel paused as she ran her pass over the pad operating the police station car park gate. It opened, allowing her to drive through and find her usual parking space. "Anyway, I'm here now. I'll be up in a minute; get the kettle on."

"Yes, boss."

Before she left her car, Rachel dialled Katie's number. "Hi, Katie. It's Detective Inspector Morrison. How are you?"

Katie's voice sounded loudly down the car phone speaker.

"I'm OK. Thank you for calling me back. I was wondering if you had any updates on my case?"

Rachel blew out her cheeks. "I'm sorry, no. I've spoken to everyone involved, but—"

"What about Bill?" Katie asked. Her tone was razor sharp.

"Bill?"

"Bill Thompson. My dad's best friend. He was there that day. He saw what happened. I went to see him recently and he shut the door in my face as soon as he realised who I was. I'm sure he knows more than he's letting on. He could be a key witness."

Rachel stifled a swear word and flicked back through her notebook. The name stared back at her, underlined several times with a question mark at the end. *How could I have forgotten to go and see him?* she thought, shaking her head.

"OK, give me his address. I'll go and pay him a visit."

She jotted down Thompson's address and ended the call with a promise to get back to Katie as soon as she had visited him. She got out of her car and headed up to her office, passing Chloe who was now back at her desk.

"Sharp, can you get me the phone number of a Bill Thompson at 35 Hancock Street, Allerton?"

"Sure. Just give me a sec." Chloe tapped the address into the computer and read out the number to Rachel who typed it into her mobile phone, then rang it. After three rings the answer machine kicked in. Rachel waited for the beep, then left her message.

"Hello, this is a message for a Mr. Bill Thompson. It's Detective Inspector Rachel Morrison calling. If you can, call me back on this number, please, or ring Merseyside Police and ask for extension 3140. Thanks." As she pressed the end call button, Jenkins appeared behind her.

"My office. Now," he said, politely but firmly. Leaving Chloe to get on with her work, she followed the simmering superintendent into his office. When she had closed the door behind her, she turned to see Jenkins' steely-blue glare trained on her.

"Sir?"

"Would you like to enlighten me as to why I've had not one, but two complaints from professional, upstanding members of our community this afternoon?"

Rachel looked blank faced, which only enraged her boss more.

"They both said they found your tone accusatory when you spoke to them, and your questions quite invasive. Care to explain?" He stood behind his desk with his hands rooted firmly on his hips, his glare not softening.

"Complaints from who?" She felt her mobile phone vibrate in her pocket.

"Martin King," Jenkins said, almost shouting. "And that vicar, Carlisle, from St Mary's in Allerton. They didn't appreciate their professional conduct being questioned, and quite frankly, Morrison, I can't blame them."

Rachel bristled and bit her lip to stop her from riposting and regretting it. She chose her words carefully. "To be honest, sir, I was concerned by the answers they gave to my legitimate questions. They seemed a little vague, so I pressed them further. Nothing more than any detective would do. Sir."

Jenkins studied her. Her reply was just on the right side of polite, but it irritated him nonetheless. He pressed his lips together and thought for a moment before continuing his tirade. "Do you remember what the ACC said? This Spencer case is to be wrapped up quickly and in *your own time*. Your preoccupation with this case has taken your focus away from the ones we're paying you good money to clear up. Chapman was in here before with her report of the ones she and Bradley have ticked off." He widened his eyes and sneered. "It comes to something when DCs are carrying a DI."

"I'm sorry, sir. I'll be wrapping the Spencer case up very soon anyway, so…"

"No, you'll wrap it up *now*, DI Morrison." Jenkins'

outburst made Rachel recoil. "And get back to what we brought you up here to do. Not opening up old wounds in this city. I'm getting enough shit on social media as it is without having to field even more complaints about the way things are done around here. We've got a reputation to rebuild in this nick. Don't you remember what ACC Clifford told you in our first meeting together? Now, you listen to me and listen good. That case is marked 'closed', so leave it be. We have enough unsolved cases to sort out without reopening closed ones." He nodded his head towards the door as a dismissal. Rachel walked back to her office feeling sore from the strip that had been torn off her.

"That sounded heavy," Chloe said, meeting her at her office door.

"Nothing I can't handle," Rachel replied, stepping inside.

"Your desk phone rang while you were in with Jenkins. Hope it was OK to answer?"

Rachel nodded. "Was it Bill Thompson?"

"Yes. Wanted to know what you wanted. A pleasant chap," Chloe added, curling her lip. She wandered back over to her desk and sat down, still watching Rachel from afar.

"Thanks." Rachel fished in her pocket for her mobile and saw a missed call from Thompson's number. He answered on the second ring.

"Yeah?" a gravelly voice greeted her

"Mr. Thompson?" Rachel asked brightly. "Bill Thompson?"

"Who's this?"

"It's Detective Inspector Rachel Morrison. I left you a voicemail earlier. I got your message to call you back."

"Did you find it, then?"

Rachel's ears pricked up. "Find what?"

"My motorbike. I reported it stolen and was told a police officer would call me back. That was a week ago. Took your time." Thompson's tone was gruff.

"No, Mr. Thompson. No. I don't work in that department.

I was calling you hoping you might be able to help me with a case I'm investigating. An old case from about twenty years ago?"

There was a heavy pause on the line. "What case?"

"The Spencer case from 2000. You were cited as a key witness. I'd just like to know what you saw that day. Could I possibly come and speak to you about it, please?"

"Why are you raking all of that up again? It's been and gone." Thompson's voice quivered. "I spoke to the police at the time."

"I know. But some new evidence has come up since then. Can you remember if there was anyone else there at the cabin shed the day Mollie Spencer died? Other than yourself, Katie, and her father?"

"No, there wasn't," Thompson sneered. "Now, if you don't mind…"

"Yes, of course. I'll let you get on. But if you're free tomorrow, I'll come over and just go over a few of the finer points. Say around 3 p.m.?"

"If you must. But there's nothing more to tell on this story. Goodbye." Thompson hung up.

"Right, he's my last hope of getting to the bottom of this case," Rachel said as Chloe appeared at her door. She ran a hand through her tousled dark hair and began chiding herself. "How could I have forgotten to go and speak to him? I don't know where my head's at sometimes."

"He didn't exactly sound like he was full of sparkling conversation," Chloe remarked, half smiling.

"No. Anyway, I really want to wrap this case up. Mum's visiting this weekend."

Chloe's face beamed. "Lovely. You planning some nice things to do together?"

"Not sure yet. Lunch probably, then maybe a walk around the Albert Dock? I've not had a proper look around there yet, and you keep banging on about how cool and hip it is there." She flashed Chloe a mock weary smile.

"A cheeky Miller and Carter, then on to Revolution bar? What's not to like? I'll take you there one night if you like? Give you the guided tour? Might even take you to the Panam if you play your cards right, boss?" Chloe added with a cheeky sidelong look as she left Rachel smiling at her desk.

Chapter 23

THE FAÇADE of 35 Hancock Street was noticeably more dilapidated than the rest of the Victorian semi-detached properties in the leafy suburban street in Allerton. Rachel pulled her car into Bill Thompson's cobbled driveway next to a battered and rusty silver Vauxhall Astra that occupied half of the driveway and half of a front garden, which was overgrown with weeds and bits of rubbish. The black paint on the wooden window frames was flaking and one of the grimy panes of glass had a hole the size of a fist in it. It looked as if a rock had been thrown through it. Rachel walked up to the front of the house, passing a little stone wishing well water feature a few yards from the black-painted wooden front door. She walked up to it and rang the doorbell. Several seconds passed without an answer so she knocked loudly using the green-speckled brass effect door knocker. She waited a few seconds more and then knocked again.

"Mr. Thompson? Are you there?" Rachel called through the letterbox. "It's Detective Inspector Morrison. Remember I said I'd be here at three? Hello?" Still nothing. She stepped back and looked around the area for options. The rubbish bins at the side of the house were overflowing with takeaway boxes and beer cans, some of which had spilled over the lip of the bin and had beetles and other bugs crawling all over then. As well as the unkempt nature of the property, Rachel caught the scent of fetid rubbish and burning in the breeze floating from down the side of the house. Curious about the latter smell, she pushed open the rickety metal side gate and walked into the back garden. There, to her horror, she saw a huge metal barrel, cut in half and raised onto a wooden stand, full to the brim of burning material. The flames licked around the rim of the barrel, kicking out plumes of thick acrid black smoke.

"Shit!"

She unwrapped the chiffon scarf she was wearing and clamped it against her face, coughing and almost choking as she got closer to see what was in the barrel. She stopped dead when she saw a petrol can next to it. She took her phone out.

"This is Detective Inspector Morrison. I'm at 35 Hancock Street, Allerton. I need the fire brigade…" As she turned around to face the back of the house, she almost dropped the phone. She suddenly realised why Bill Thompson hadn't answered his front door.

"And an ambulance. *Now.*"

Facing the open back door of the conservatory, her eyes were drawn up to the lintel above the doorway into the house. There she saw the grim sight of Bill Thompson's hanging corpse. A wooden stool was lying on its side underneath his dangling legs. His bloated and grotesque face was blue and veiny, his dead eyes wide and staring, and mottled with tiny red specks. The chafing mark from the rope around his neck was as red and angry-looking as the fire that was now raging behind her.

———

THE FIRE HAD BEEN RELATIVELY easy to put out, once the fire brigade had assessed the scene and set to it. Scene of crime officers moved carefully and methodically around the house and garden, wearing white zip-up suits, face masks, and blue coverings over their shoes. One officer walked past Rachel carrying five square plastic tiles, laying one at the entrance to the conservatory and the next one on the dirty grey floor tile in the entrance in front of her. Two uniformed police officers stood at the side gate, lifting the yellow and black crime scene tape for attending officers, two of whom were approaching Rachel now.

"What the hell is going on here?" Jenkins roared. His combed-back grey hair shook with the force of his voice. His eyes fixed Rachel with his hardest stare. Behind him was the welcome sight of DC Chloe Sharp. She mouthed 'are you OK?' to Rachel, who nodded.

"Suicide, sir."

"I can see that, *Detective Inspector* Morrison," he spat back, emphasising her rank in a sneering tone. "I've been on the force for twenty-seven years. I know what a suicide looks like. What I want to know is why you are here."

"I called it in." Rachel jutted her head towards the now-smouldering charred barrel. "There was a fire, so I investigated. That's when I saw Thompson's body."

Jenkins pressed his face close to Rachel's, covering her with his stale coffee breath. "I know that too, Morrison. What I want to know is why you are here in the first place."

Taking a step back, Rachel looked him full in the face. "I had some questions I wanted to ask Thompson. About the Mollie Spencer case. Just before I wrap it up," she added, as Jenkins was about to rail against her. "He agreed to see me, but just before I got here, he topped himself."

"He was probably suffering from PTSD, and here you come, bowling in, raking up something terrible from his past that has been closed by the *fucking* police. Have you got no sense? This might be how you do things in the Met, or even down in Cornwall. But it's not how my coppers behave." He stepped closer again, checking around him to make sure no one could hear him. "Now you listen to me. Both I and Clifford told you to drop this case and get on with what you're paid to do. But you are constantly disobeying us. You will stop this. Now."

"Why was he burning things?" Rachel said. Jenkins recoiled.

"What?"

"In the barrel. It is full of charred remains of clothes, photographs. There's even what looks like videotapes in there. I'll have it all bagged, of course. But why would someone, with nothing to hide, burn loads of personal effects just before a police officer comes around to speak to him about a death he witnessed?"

"Are the videotapes playable?" Jenkins asked, his tone softer.

"I don't know yet. I'll send them to the lab. But the fire was accelerated with petrol, so I doubt it."

Jenkins was stuck in thought for a moment. "Go home, Rachel. You have a few days' leave owing. I suggest you take them. Now."

———

No SOONER HAD Supt. Jenkins returned to his office and thrown his coat and police hat down on his cluttered desk, ACC Clifford stormed in behind him.

"Is what I'm hearing correct? Morrison is still disobeying orders?"

Jenkins shook a weary head and exhaled at length.

Clifford set his lips and put his hands on his hips. "I allocated a budget to put to bed misper cases that have clogged up that archives room for years, and try and get this force's reputation back on track. Tell me, why on earth is that budget getting blown on cases already closed?"

"Sir, if I could just explain…"

"First the complaints from the vicar and the therapist,

then I hear about this suicide. This 'supercop' I was promised is becoming a bit of a liability."

"I know that. I've sent her home. She needs to reassess her priorities."

Clifford balked. "You've sent her home?"

"Yes. I thought it was best. Cool her off a bit. Give her some thinking time."

"Great," Clifford bellowed. "So, not only am I paying for her to investigate cases that I never asked her to, but now I am paying for her to sit on her behind at home?"

Jenkins swallowed hard, realising Clifford made a sound point.

"It's *you* that needs the thinking time, Graham. If this all goes tits up, I will be blaming you." Clifford's booming voice reverberated around Jenkins' office, matched only by his heavy footsteps as he marched out, slamming the door behind him.

Chapter 24

THE WEATHER FORECAST was pleasantly accurate for that Saturday morning, so Rachel thought as she sat on a bench in the middle of Sefton Park. The sun was warm on the back of her neck, the wind light and ruffling up her light yellow summer dress. She had picked her mum up on Friday evening from Lime Street and spent the evening talking over the events of the last few weeks since Rachel had moved up. Now, after a hearty breakfast at a café in Lark Lane, and a meander around the Palm House, mother and daughter sat in the park watching a group of pigeons fighting over a scrap of sandwich a picnicker had dropped moments before.

"Are you OK, love?" Rachel's mum asked, after staring at her profile for a few silent minutes. The concern in her light blue eyes was tangible. She was in her mid-sixties, her greying hair a similar length now to Rachel's. She was wearing a pale green dress and light summer jacket. By her side was a white tote bag containing her purse and a couple of bottles of orange juice.

"Yeah, fine," Rachel sighed. Her gaze was fixed on the expansive lush green grass as far as the eye could see. A group of cyclists were trundling along the far perimeter path, clad in

189

bright green and yellow Lycra. She couldn't help but wonder if Chloe Sharp was among them. "Just a lot going on at work. Nothing new there then," she added, smiling sidelong at her mother.

"Are you enjoying the job? Being up here?"

"I guess so. It's not forever, is it? And it's a change of scene. You always said that would be good for me." Her thoughts drifted back to the note that had been left on her car windscreen just before she'd left Lizard. *I know what you did. Don't worry, it's our little secret.* To this day, she still had no idea who had left the note. Could it have been from someone caught up in Amanda Walker's trail of destruction? The mystery of it had often kept her awake at night, sometimes even had her waking up in a cold sweat after a particularly vivid dream about the day Amanda had her head blasted open. Being hundreds of miles away had taken the sting out of the words in the note, but Rachel still couldn't help but feel a cloying sense of pressure around her. Especially lately.

"I don't know where I fit in anymore, Mum. I don't know what I came here looking for."

"To make a difference. It's your motivation in everything you do. Has been since you were little."

"But with this latest case, all I've done is cause destruction. I feel like I'm losing my judgement." She exhaled at length. Her mother clamped a well-manicured hand over hers. Rachel continued, "I don't know why I came up here, Mum. Was it because I was running away from the situation with Adam because it was too painful to deal with in our home? Or was it because I needed to feel the same high of the praise I was getting for solving the Kynance Cove murders? I don't know who I am anymore, or what I want. My head is such a mess."

"Even if you were doing it for the praise from the bosses, or the adoration from the young pups of the force," her mother said in a soothing voice, "that doesn't make you a bad person. There are worse things in life to be motivated by than wanting to do a good job and wanting people to like and appreciate you for it. People will love and respect you for who you are, not what it says on your badge. You just need to open up to people more. Make some friends. Now Adam's gone, you might even meet someone who makes you smile again."

Rachel exhaled at length, her eyes fixed on the horizon and the little group of cyclists.

———

"How was your weekend with your mum?" Chloe Sharp's bright voice piped up over the top of her cubicle partition as Rachel swished past her.

"Lovely, thanks. I've just dropped her off at Lime Street for the early train home." Rachel's smile was wide but it hadn't reached her eyes. Chloe noticed.

"You seem a bit down. I bet you were sad to see her go."

"No, it's not that. I just feel I've neglected you all, while I've been banging the doors down on the Spencer case." She looked at Chloe with keen eyes. "I should have been paying more attention to you. And Bradley and Mags," she added.

Chloe felt a warmth rush to her cheeks. Suppressing it, she grinned. "Well then, neglect us no longer, boss. Let's get cracking."

"Excellent. Go and muster the troops and tell them I'd like a catch up in five minutes in my office. I just need to make a call to Katie to tell her about Thompson, and that we're closing the case for good this time."

"Good," Chloe said, nodding. "She needs to put this all behind her. The past is past. Everyone is entitled to a fresh start." She held Rachel's gaze for a moment before turning and heading over to DC Bradley's desk to tell him about the meeting.

———

Katie's phone had vibrated against the dashboard and after seeing it was Rachel calling, she fumbled across the seat to reach it, pulling the wheel as she did so.

"Hello? Rachel?"

The car swerved, causing Katie to drop the phone with a thud into the passenger side footwell. She fought to right the car. It swerved the other way and skidded along the grass verge of the main road. With her foot stamped hard into the brake, Katie grimaced as a tree appeared large in front of the car. Bracing herself for the impact, she closed her eyes and smashed into the thick trunk of the oak. The car now crushed in at the bonnet and smoking from the engine bay, Katie lifted her head from the air bag that had deployed and cushioned her impact into the steering wheel. Her phone had stopped vibrating now, and the back light was now dark. Groaning, Katie put her shaking hand to her forehead and felt the warm sticky liquid that had pooled on her skin, matting her hair down. She broke into a fit of sobs, shrieking at the silent air around the deserted road.

"Why can't I remember? Why can't I remember?"

Unbuckling her seatbelt, wincing as she did so, she tried to reach down to the footwell to retrieve her phone, but in lowering her head, the blood rushed forward and sent her into a faint. She slumped against the seat, the drips of blood from the gash in her forehead pooling on the centre console.

———

Waiting for the beep, Rachel composed her message in her head. "Hi Katie, it's Detective Inspector Morrison. If you could call me back when you get this message. Thanks, bye." She pressed the end call button just as Chloe Sharp burst into her office, her characteristically buoyant face now serious.

"There's somebody here to see you, boss. Says it's urgent and he won't talk to anyone else but you."

Rachel looked up wearily, rubbing her eyes. "Who is it?"

"Robbie Reynolds. He said he's ready to talk."

Chapter 25

WITH HER HEART in her mouth, Rachel flew down the stairs from the incident room to reception. Robbie Reynolds sat there, wearing the same dirty jeans and wool jumper he'd worn the day Rachel met him up on his nan's farm. He looked up at her, his face an unshaven mess.

"Robbie, hi. How are you?" Rachel said. She reached out her hand to shake his, but he remained staring at her. "Shall we go and find a quiet room?" Leading the way, Rachel sat Robbie down in an interview room just behind the front desk. She slid the vacant sign on the door over to make sure she wasn't disturbed.

"Can I have a drink of water, please?" Robbie said. He licked his dry lips and coughed.

"Sure."

Rachel filled a beaker from the water cooler next to the door and placed it on the table in front of Robbie, who had now sat down. He put his trembling hands on his knees and swallowed hard, before taking a huge swig from the beaker of water. He coughed again and wiped his mouth with a dirt-encrusted sleeve.

"Why are you here, Robbie?" Rachel asked. She had

taken her seat opposite him and was now looking at him with keen brown eyes.

"I saw in the paper that the investigation into Mollie Spencer's death might be reopened. I remember the first investigation, and how shit it was handled." His voice was shaky, his scouse accent more prominent now than it had been back when she'd met him in Scotland. "I can't let that poor girl go through this anymore."

Rachel leaned forward. "What are you talking about, Robbie?"

He looked up from the table, his stare now hard. "I know Katie got the blame for Mollie's death. Everyone in the street thought it was her. But the papers weren't allowed to print anything, and Katie was sent away. They hoped it would all go away, just reporting it as accidental death." He clenched his teeth. "But it wasn't an accident." He paused and looked down at the table, his fists now clenched. "Mollie was murdered. And it's all my fault."

"Robbie?" Rachel prompted.

"Katie Spencer did not kill her sister. I know because I was there."

———

RACHEL RETURNED to the interview room with a strong black coffee which she'd put four large sachets of sugars in. As soon as Robbie had told her about Mollie's death being murder, he'd broken down into a fit of hysterical crying, throwing the chair back and crouching in the corner like a wounded animal. Letting him calm down, she left the door open to keep an eye on him while she popped into the corridor to get him a drink. The desk sergeant flashed her a concerned glance, as if to ask her if she needed back up, but she waved it away. She looked back into the room and saw Robbie now standing and picking up the chair to slot it back underneath the table. He sat down as if his outburst had never happened.

"Here you go. Careful, it's hot," Rachel said, putting the beaker of coffee in front of him. Robbie stared at it but left it untouched. "Robbie, can you tell me what happened the day Mollie died?"

Robbie took a deep breath. "Me and Katie were mates growing up. Her older sister, Jenny was a bit of a cow, but I liked Katie. Not as stuck up as Jenny. Katie was dead nice to me when my parents were kicking me around. She got me food when they didn't feed me, that kind of thing. She was so kind. She wouldn't hurt a fly."

"Go on," Rachel said, seeing Robbie drift off into his memories. He refocused his eyes and came right out with it.

"Katie didn't kill Mollie. Bill Thompson did."

———

"Where is DI Morrison, Sharp?" Jenkins asked.

Chloe turned around from her computer and thought carefully about lying to a superior officer. "Not sure, sir. She received a call a while ago and disappeared, but I haven't seen her since," she replied, her answer just on the right side of truthful. Jenkins scowled and slunk away back to his office.

"What's crawled up his arse today?" Mags said, plonking herself down in the seat opposite.

"Oh, he's just on the warpath. The boss has been digging into the Spencer case on company time and he's not happy about it."

Mags made a face. "Well, to be honest, he has got a point. I mean, here we are slaving away on cases she's supposed to be boxing off. I dread to think the money they've shelled out to drag her up here from Cornwall."

"I think she just wants some closure for Katie Spencer. In a way that's another case boxed off, even if it's not one of ours."

"She's really won you over, hasn't she, Chloe? See yourself like her in a few years' time, I'll bet?"

Chloe looked back at her computer, ignoring Mags' jibe. Realising she wasn't getting a reaction, Mags got up and walked away. "I can think of worse people in this office to aspire to," Chloe whispered to herself.

———

RACHEL STARED AT ROBBIE, her mind fizzing with what she'd just heard. She swallowed and leaned forward, interlacing her fingers. "What happened, Robbie? Take me back to that day."

Robbie squirmed in his chair, as if the memory of it were eating into his brain like a pack of carnivorous ants.

"Back when I was a boy, I did work for Bill Thompson and Peter Spencer. They paid my parents direct, cash in hand. Never to me. They probably thought I would spend it on sweets and shit. Which, to be fair, I probably would. So, my parents started getting used to the income. They were never what you would call 'honest workers'. There was always some kind of benefit fraud going on with them. They knew how to play the system. People like that always do."

"So, they kept forcing me to go over to Peter's house. Bill was pretty much there all the time anyway. He wasn't married and didn't have any children of his own, so he had nothing better to do. They hung around mostly in the cabin shed at the bottom of Peter's garden, watching footie and drinking cans. It's right out of the way of the house. And out of earshot."

He paused and licked his lips. Taking a thirsty sip from the coffee, he composed his thoughts and began again.

"When I was about ten years old, Bill asked me one day to help him to do some repairs on the cabin shed. Nothing major. Just picking up nails that fell through the slats and onto the ground below. I'd be quicker than if he had to stop all the time and pick them up. He didn't want his dog treading on them or eating them or whatever shit reason it was that he gave me at the time. But it was really hot one day and I was getting fidgety, running around in my jumper and jeans, so Bill…" Robbie broke off as his eyes became glassy. "Bill suggested I take off my jumper and jeans and work in my boxer shorts. Said I might even get a tan, so I wouldn't look so pasty white."

Rachel pressed her lips together and fought the urge to close her eyes and shake her head.

"Bill and Peter used to stand over me while I bent down to pick the nails up from underneath the decking. One time I looked back up to see them both leering at me like…" He paused again, unable to say the word. "As I got more tanned from being outside all the time, they used to say that all the girls would like me at school because of it. I was only ten, for fuck's sake. What the hell did I know about girls? But I know now they were flattering me so I would like *them* more. And with my own dad beating me every time he felt like it, I did. Their place was my safe place, or so I thought. I actually did start to like Bill and Peter."

"Day by day, little things started to happen. They would say things like, 'let us show you what boys and girls do together to help you get prepped', and 'when girls do this to you, it feels really nice'. That was the first day Bill gave me oral sex."

Robbie pulled his cuffs over his wrists and wrapped his arms around himself. He shook his head as if to try and erase the memory, which he was clearly replaying.

"Then Peter did the same thing the following day. I told them I didn't want them to do it. But they laughed and called me a wimp. Said they'd stop giving my parents money for all the work I was doing. They said if I told anyone what they were doing, then they'd call the police and tell them I'd been stealing from them. I'd already been in a bit of trouble by then, so I was terrified. So there I was, twice a week, packed off down the road to Bill and Peter, for them to do what they liked to me, just so I could take money home to my useless fucking parents, who were too lazy to get a job themselves.

Then it got worse for me. They asked me how it felt when they gave me oral sex, and that it was time for me to do it on them. Said it was only fair they get some back, for all the money they were paying. I didn't have a clue what to do, but they forced me to do it anyway. They said if I did it really well, then I'd get a 'bonus'. They would just tell Mum and Dad I'd worked extra hard around the garden that day."

Bastards, Rachel thought. "How long did this carry on for, Robbie?" she said softly.

"For the rest of that summer, the cabin shed got a bit more built up the more work they did on it. They'd had it insulated and set up a TV and all that. Then they started to film what I was doing to them. And what they were doing to me. They started bending me over the table and taking turns to…" Robbie couldn't say the word. He closed his eyes and shuddered. "One would do it, the other would film it. They told me I was making a lot of people happy with what I was doing. I didn't know what they meant at the time. But obviously people must have been watching it somehow. But I felt nothing but disgust."

"Was there no one you could tell, Robbie? Other than your parents, was there no one? A teacher?"

"No. I had a reputation of telling stories when I was a little kid. I was an only child. No one to talk to at school so I used to make things up all the time to get attention. I wanted people to like me because life was so shit at home. But people used to roll their eyes at me. So they would have just thought I was attention seeking, as usual. I didn't dare say anything because I was ashamed. How do you come out and say you regularly get molested by some old ugly smelly bastards?"

The tears were let loose from Robbie's eyes. He covered his face with his hands and sobbed. Rachel reached over the table and held his arm.

"What happened the day Mollie died?"

Robbie lifted his face and wiped it with his hand. He sniffed and attempted to compose himself.

"Bill and Peter told my parents to send me over to finish a job for them. Said there was fifty quid in it for them if they could have me for the whole day. Of course, they said yes. I never told them what was really going on. I didn't dare. What would have been the point? I was keeping them in booze and weed, so I doubt they'd even have given a shit. I wanted to run away, and by then I think I'd just become numb to it all. But this one time, it was just disgusting. The cabin had been cleaned and I wasn't allowed to wear my trainers in there, so I took them off before I went inside. I left them outside the door. When I got in the cabin shed, Bill and Peter had set the camera up on a tripod so neither of them had to operate it. There was some cable thing with a button on it they could press so it would start recording. They wanted to…to…"

Robbie stopped and leaned over the table as if he were about to vomit. He retched a few times, before sitting back upright.

"They wanted to try and have me at the same time. One behind me and one in front. I remember thinking, 'how is that even possible?' But they grabbed me and threw me over the table. It was the first time they'd been proper rough with me and I fought back. But they were so strong. Bill ripped my trousers down and before I knew what was happening he was…you know. I screamed in pain. I knew no one would hear. Then my screams stopped. Peter made sure of that when he filled my mouth with his dick. I gagged. I couldn't breathe. And then Bill heard a noise outside the cabin shed window."

———

SUPT. JENKINS SAT at his desk, drumming his fingers on the surface. In front of him was his monthly report of the solved case ratio and it didn't make for comfortable reading. Mags and Bradley had made a dent in the massive pile of folders in Rachel's office, but Rachel and Chloe had been caught up in the Spencer case for far too many weeks now. With ACC

Clifford awaiting his run-down of how well the budget had been spent that month on resources, and Rachel nowhere to be seen to explain her poor performance, Jenkins' anger was spilling over. As he looked up at the clock on the wall, the feeling of dread for the meeting that was about to commence was building by the second. He could almost hear Clifford's heavy footsteps making their way over to him from his office.

"She was told, they were all told, forbidden even, from going anywhere near the cabin shed at any time. They should have listened. Why didn't they listen?" Robbie's eyes were like saucers, his hands spread in disbelief.

"You mean the girls? Mollie, Katie and Jenny?" Rachel asked.

"Yes. Bill looked up after he heard the noise and saw Mollie's face staring in the window looking straight at him while he was doing what he was doing to me. She must have been so confused. Peter turned around and saw her too. She'd seen everything. Her little eyes. I shouted to her to help me, to get help. But she was five years old, for fuck's sake! She didn't understand *what* was happening to me, other than I was being hurt. She kept shouting through the net curtains in the window, 'You're hurting Robbie, Daddy. You're hurting Robbie, Uncle Bill'."

"Bill threw me forward and I fell from the table onto the floor. All I heard next was Peter shouting to get Mollie. I looked out the window and they ran out to the decking and the next I saw was Bill grab Mollie really rough while Peter was doing his trousers up. Mollie screamed for help and Bill shook her so hard that it alone would have broken her neck. He pushed her as she tried to run from him. I saw him do it. She fell off the decking, cracking her neck on the way down from a corner of the steps. Then the thud. I'll never forget that cracking sound. I hear it in my nightmares. Mollie's skull smashing against that rock underneath the cabin shed."

Robbie's face creased and he retched again. Rachel pushed the coffee towards him and he took a gulp.

"I peeked around from the opened door of the cabin. I saw Katie coming over and looking at where Mollie had fallen and then screaming. God, what a sight that must have been. Peter and Bill were now looking down from the decking at Mollie in horror. Then, I'll never forget the moment when they looked at each other and then down at Katie. Bill said, 'You did this, Katie. You pushed your sister. She's dead. She's dead, Katie. Somebody help!' He shouted it so the neighbours could hear. I saw Jenny come rushing over, looking at Katie and screaming. What was she supposed to think? Then the neighbours arrived, after hearing the screams."

"What did you do, Robbie?" Rachel asked.

"I grabbed my trainers and jumped down off the decking at the back, around the other side to where Mollie had fallen, and ran. I just wanted to get out of there. I ran as fast as I could. Like I said before, I had a reputation of telling tales. I couldn't tell the police what had happened and what I'd seen. I was scared they would kill me like they killed Mollie. I was trapped. I didn't know what to do. I thought, hoped, the police would do their fucking job and interview all of the witnesses, other than me, and piece together what had happened. Like you see on the telly. But all that happened was Katie got the blame and Bill and Peter got to carry on as before. I felt so guilty, but there was no one else I could think of to tell."

"But you told *someone*, didn't you? When I first met you, up in Scotland, you said you'd told someone. It was Reverend Carlisle, wasn't it?"

Robbie fixed Rachel with a hard stare. "You know when you're told as a kid to tell an adult you can trust if there is something that is bothering you? Well, I didn't have many adults like that. So I ran to the church across the road from our street, and found the vicar.”

“I used to do some work for him. Proper work. He treated me well, gave me food when I was hungry. Reverend Carlisle saw me running through the lichgate and grabbed me. Told me to calm down and tell him what was troubling me. I’ll never forget the look on his face when I told him what Bill and Peter were doing to me. And what they’d done to Mollie. Somehow he convinced me that because Bill and Peter had done so much for the church, helping replace the roof and contributing to the church fundraisers every year, that I must be mistaken.”

Lying bastard, Rachel thought, thinking back to her conversation with Reverend Carlisle.

“I realised then that I couldn’t trust him. So, after I’d thought about it a bit more, I went to the last place I could think of for help, where even if they *didn’t* believe me, they would have to investigate. I went to the police station and spoke to a copper there. I told them everything I could. They said they appreciated me coming down and they’d get back to me as soon as they’d investigated. I should have known they wouldn’t. They didn’t even take any notes.”

“When I went home, I got the beating of my life. Reverend Carlisle had rung my parents and told them what I’d told him. I was up in my bedroom afterwards, listening to my mum and dad argue about what they were going to do to me to shut me up, and the next minute a stone came flying through my window. I looked out and there was a lad I knew from Hancock Street standing outside. Mikey Miller, his name was. He was a bit older, seventeen, I think. He had a rucksack with him. I’d seen him before, around the cabin shed and it dawned on me that he might be able to corroborate what I’d said. But he didn’t want to stay around and take the chance that someone would believe him. Bill and Peter had been abusing him for years. He shouted up to me to pack a bag and showed me a big wad of money he'd stolen from his dad's wallet. So I did."

"I packed a bag and got on the first train out of Liverpool. Mikey only went as far as Lime Street with me. He got on a train there to the airport, planning to go to Spain where his uncle lived, and I set off on one up to Preston, and then on to Scotland. Ten-year-old me, on a train all alone. But I managed to avoid the train staff. I knew from the address book I nicked from Mum that my nan lived up in Crailach so I headed there. The taxi that took me up to her farmhouse from the village station liked the colour of my money so didn't ask too many questions. I had Nan's photo and recognised her immediately when she came to the door."

"Nan rang Mum and Dad to let them know I was safe, even though I asked her not to. It was a compromise, I think." He lifted his eyes to Rachel and broke from his recollection. "And then all these years later, you show up and start asking questions. Telling me you were looking into Mollie Spencer's death. It all came flooding back to me. I was sick after you left. My nan was well worried. Then I read online that the case might be reopened, and I couldn't let what Bill and Peter did haunt me any longer. I knew I had to tell the truth finally. About what happened to me, to Mikey, and all of those other boys."

Rachel sat up straight. "There's more?"

"Of course. Who do you think Bill and Peter were sending the videos to? There's a massive group of paedos involved in this. Mikey told me of at least thirty names of boys he knew of being abused. He saw the shelves in the cabin shed full of videotapes with name labels on. Said that Bill had loads at his house too. He must have over twenty years' worth of footage now, the dirty bastard."

Rachel remembered the barrel fire she'd seen at Bill's house when she found his body. *He must have panicked when he knew I was coming over to talk to him about the case and burned any evidence he had*, she thought.

"Me and Mikey? We're just the tip of the iceberg. The men watching these videos, they are all over the country, doing to other boys what Bill and Peter were doing to Mikey and me. Some boys that Bill and Peter abused were from around the town. Some were just other waifs and strays that the older boys that were being abused used to bring along to the cabin shed with them."

"Robbie, do you remember Bill or Peter mentioning any of these other men by name? Or where they were located?" Rachel took out her notebook for the first time and sat with her pen poised. Robbie shook his head.

"No. I can't speak for nowadays, but back then they were just referred to by code names. But I don't remember any. I was only ten, remember, so a lot of it is hazy. It comes back to me sometimes in my nightmares, but as soon as I wake up it's gone. Mikey might know, because he was older, but I don't have an address for him in Spain. The last time I saw him was at Lime Street station when we parted ways all those years ago."

A thought suddenly popped into Rachel's head. "This is a long shot, Robbie. But does the name Callum Davies mean anything to you?"

Robbie nodded. "Mikey said Callum got it pretty bad. He tried to escape a couple of times. Callum's dad was making money from sending Callum to the cabin. What animal does that to his own kid? No idea where Callum is now, though. He'd be a year or two older than me now."

"OK, Robbie. I'm going to need you to do a formal statement. So we can exonerate Katie," Rachel said.

Robbie nodded and broke down in inconsolable sobs. His nightmare of holding the truth inside all these years was finally over.

But Rachel knew now that there were so many more out there, like Robbie, who had gone through and were going through unimaginable horror. She exhaled at length, realising she had only just scratched the surface.

Epilogue

Tom brought Katie her third cup of tea in the space of an hour. He had brought her home from the hospital that morning, a bump on her head the only tangible injury from her car accident. He sat next to her on the sofa and wrapped a purple fleece throw around her legs.

"I'm fine, Tom. Stop fussing," Katie said, wriggling under his touch.

"You gave me a right scare before. Of course I'm going to fuss."

"No harm done, really. Just a little cut. The car's fine."

"Sod the car." He broke off as Katie's mobile phone rang. It was Rachel.

"Hello?" Katie said. She listened in silence until Rachel said the magic words she'd been waiting the last few weeks to hear. Crying with relief, she thanked Rachel and hung up the phone.

"What is it?" Tom asked, his eyes wide.

"It's been confirmed, Tom. I didn't do it. I didn't kill Mollie." She sank into his arms and sobbed.

Katie was convinced Jenny still wouldn't believe her, so had asked Rachel to ring her and confirm the news. A week later, Katie's whole world felt brighter. Raising her head to breathe in the warm, salty Brighton air, she stood in her front garden and set about watering the new plants she'd bought. They were blooming now, with bright pink and red petals, but her attention was drawn to the taxi that had pulled up outside her house. Her jaw slackened with shock when she saw who stepped out of it.

"Jenny? What are you doing here?" she said, staring at her sister. She was wearing a light summer jacket, blue jeans and a pink t-shirt. Crawling out of the car seat next to her was Charlotte, wearing a beautiful lemon yellow summer dress. She was still holding on to the black and tan dog teddy she'd had the last time Katie saw her. Jenny's face melted into tears.

"Oh, Katie. I am so sorry." She rushed over to throw her arms around Katie, with Charlotte running behind to hug Katie's legs. "I don't know how you can ever forgive me for the way I've been. I know the truth now."

Katie prised her face away from Jenny's shoulder. "It doesn't matter now. All that matters is that we try and be a family. Can we?" Katie's eyes filled with hope that, for once, Jenny's smiling face confirmed.

"What's going on?" Tom asked. He stood in the doorway looking confused at the embrace Katie, Jenny and Charlotte were wrapped up in. Timmy appeared behind him and ran over to Charlotte, who bent down and patted him. She showed him her dog teddy.

Katie hugged Jenny closer to her and looked over to Tom, who was watching and laughing at Charlotte's strange little conversation with Timmy. He smiled back at her and mouthed, I love you.

Katie looked to the heavens and smiled, with one thought in her head. *I just wish you were here, Auntie Joan. But I'm going to be OK now.*

CHLOE SHARP STOOD at Rachel's office door. She was sitting staring down at her phone.

"You OK?"

"Yeah. Just been looking at that photo on Adam's Facebook again," Rachel replied, frowning. "I mean, they *could* just be friends."

Chloe gave her a sympathetic smile. "I don't pose for photos like *that* with my friends. You shouldn't torture yourself. He's the arsehole." Realising who she was speaking to, and where she was, Chloe stopped talking. "Sorry, boss."

"No, it's fine. You're right."

Rachel threw her phone down on the desk, hitting a large plastic evidence bag, full of charred remains of what looked like paper that took most of the space in front of her.

"What's all that?" Chloe said, wrinkling her nose at the weird smell.

"The stuff Bill Thompson was attempting to destroy in that barrel fire. Forensics have just brought it up for me."

"What did they find?" Chloe asked, stepping closer and poking the bag with the end of her pencil.

"Nothing I can make out. Just loads of half-burned photographs. The faces have been cut out, though, so there's no way we can identify any of the abuse victims. The background is definitely some kind of shed, though. You can tell by the wooden slats. But not much else to go on." She sighed and sat back in her chair.

"I thought this case was closed?" Chloe said, confused by the look of defeat on Rachel's tired, strained face.

Rachel looked up at Chloe, her brown eyes fixing her with a sharp stare. "After what Robbie told us, God knows what we'll find in this mess." She paused and shook her head.

"Get that coffee on, Sharp. We've uncovered a monster."

Feedback

Thank you for reading 'We Don't Speak About Mollie'. We hope you enjoyed the book? Please now scan the QR code below to leave your feedback.

Grab your free book NOW

The Nurse. The Teacher. The Gardener.

You have motive. You have means. Do you take the opportunity? Three innocent people from completely different walks of life are presented with an impossible decision. DOWNLOAD FREE: www.hackneyandjones.com

Ok, so how do I get my FREE book?

EASY! See the next page

Grab your free book NOW

Instructions:

1. Open the camera or the QR reader application on your smartphone.

2. Point your camera at the QR code to scan the QR code.

3. A notification will pop-up on screen.

4. Click on the notification to open the website link

Book 1: The Burying Place

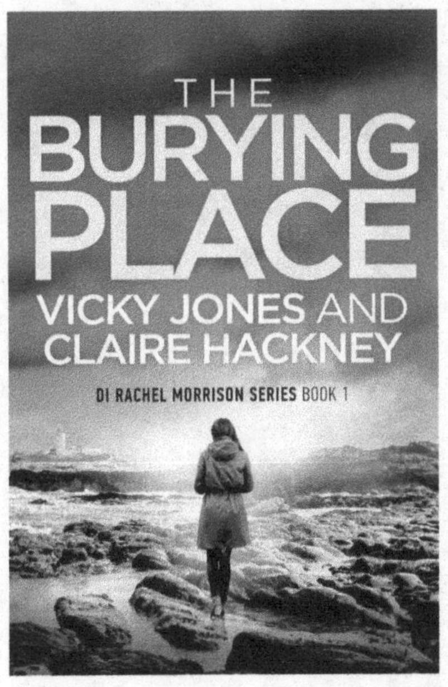

One high-profile case. No leads. No witnesses. No body. Amanda Walker's mother is missing. Detective Inspector Rachel Morrison has no leads on the case and time is running out. Amanda appeals to the public, but when no one comes forward, she chooses to immerse herself within a murderous underground group she believes is responsible for her mother's disappearance. But will the group believe Amanda's cover story?

Grab your free book NOW

Instructions:

1. Open the camera or the QR reader application on your smartphone.

2. Point your camera at the QR code to scan the QR code.

3. A notification will pop-up on screen.

4. Click on the notification to open the website link

Join in!

If you would like to receive regular behind-the-scenes updates, get beta reading opportunities, enter giveaways and much, much more, simply visit the site below:

http://hackneyandjones.com

www.ingramcontent.com/pod-product-compliance
Lightning Source LLC
Chambersburg PA
CBHW010541170726
48285CB00008B/2704